DARED

USA TODAY & WALL STREET JOURNAL BESTSELLING AUTHOR
BECCA STEELE

Dared

Editing by One Love Editing

Proofreading by Rumi

Becca Steele

www.authorbeccasteele.com

AUTHOR'S NOTE

The author is British, and this story contains British English spellings and phrases. The football referred to in this story is known as soccer in some countries.

For Jodi

Breathe, darling. This is just a chapter. It's not your whole story.

S. C. LOURIE

LEO

PROLOGUE

AGE TEN

"Hahaha! It's the stuttering ginger kid!"

I gritted my teeth, breathing through the hurt as several loud whispers and stifled laughs echoed around me. Why was it acceptable to be so horrible to another kid for something they were born with? Something they had no control over?

I didn't even *have* a stutter. I just... When I was in front of people, my nerves overtook me. I froze up, and my mouth and brain and lungs didn't always work properly together. It wasn't like I could help it, any more than I could help my hair being the way it was. And anyway, I *liked* my hair. I liked the reds and golds and hints of brown. It reminded me of my mum. She'd died when I was a baby. My dad had never really shown much of an interest in me, and that was okay because I knew I reminded him of her, and it was painful. But I'd talked him into showing me photos of my mum, and I knew we shared the same hair. It was my link to her.

A lump came into my throat, and I blinked rapidly. *Please. Please don't freeze up. Get through this, and then you can sit down and be invisible again.*

"He's gonna freeze!" The excited, high-pitched voice came from my left, immediately shushed by the teacher, but it was too late. I'd already heard it.

Staring down at the paper in my shaking hand, I bit down on my lip, staring at the words that were blurring on the page. My entire body was trembling as I opened my mouth, a fast, shallow breath escaping. "Sh-Shakespeare wrote R-Romeo and J-Juliet in—"

"Look at him!" This voice was gleeful, and I swallowed around the lump in my throat, the lump that had increased in size ever since I'd been forced to stand in front of the class and read out my homework assignment.

I licked my cracked, dry lips. It had to be obvious to everyone that I'd lost control of my emotions. My throat felt like it was closing up. "I-in—"

"He's gonna cry!"

Against my will, a tear trickled down my cheek and then another. The paper fell to the floor as the whispers closed in on me, the laughter growing louder.

The teacher rushed to the front of the room, reprimanding the class and ushering me back to my seat, but it was too late. I buried my face in my arms, digging my teeth into my left bicep in an attempt to stifle my sobs. My shoulders shook as the tears fell hot and fast with the eyes of my classmates on me, there to witness me falling apart.

ONE

LEO

Reclining back in my gaming chair, I rolled my ankles in slow circles as I browsed through the new *Lesath Legends* in-game armour that had just dropped. As I was equipping my character with a new shield, I heard the front door slam, and a minute later, my flatmate, Connor, was poking his head around my bedroom door.

"Alright? What you up to? I'm gonna be recording for my channel for the next couple of hours, then I have a Twitch stream at nine."

That was Connor-speak for "do not disturb me while I work on my online content." It was the main reason we made good flatmates. That, and the fact we were both studying for a computing degree. Connor was so different from me—confident and outgoing, but he needed peace and quiet to make his content. When he'd discovered my love for endless hours of gaming when I wasn't occupied with my uni work, he'd asked if I wanted to split the rent with him on a flat he'd found close to campus. I'd already resigned myself to living alone or having to share a house with strangers, as I'd done in my first year of uni, so his offer had come as a complete surprise. But when he'd promised me he was serious, I'd happily accepted.

"I'll just be here gaming, anyway." Stretching my legs out with a groan, I continued. "I don't want to move for the next few hours. Dance practice killed me today."

Shaking his head, Connor grinned at me. "You brought it all on yourself, bro. Who combines a computing major with a dance minor? Only you. Take me, for example. A far more sensible combination of visual communication and computing." He shook his head. "Then again, you get to hang out with hot dancers. Maybe I could get an intro sometime. If they're hot and single, send them my way."

"Yeah...maybe." It wasn't that I didn't want him to meet my dance friends. It was just that I only had two I could really call friends, and both were in relationships. Connor knew I was shy and struggled with anything social or being in the spotlight, but I felt a bit...humiliated, I guess, that we were drawing closer to the end of the second year of our degrees, and I'd made friends with a grand total of two people on my dance course. It was more or less the same story with my computing major—I had Connor and another friend called Niall, who I usually teamed up with for group projects, but there wasn't anyone else I properly hung out with.

I wished I could be normal.

Connor nodded, rapping his knuckles on the door frame as he straightened up. "Don't even worry about it. I'm gonna go and get set up. If you get hungry later, there's still some of that pizza in the fridge. I only had a couple of slices for lunch."

"Thanks." I smiled at him, grateful that he understood and always seemed to know when to back off. "Good luck with your things."

"You too. Have fun killing monsters. Y'know, you could get a decent Twitch following if you live-streamed your games, make some money out of it."

"Not happening."

"It was worth a try."

I winced. "Sorry." Every now and then, he'd try to get me to do something outside of my comfort zone, rarely succeeding, but he didn't give up or take offence when I said no.

He grinned at me. "You know I'm gonna keep trying." With a salute, he disappeared, and I settled myself at my desk, ready to play *Lesath Legends*.

A message popped up in the chat window, and a smile spread across my face. Hammerhead was online.

HAMMERHEAD:

Want to play duos? See if we can get the limited-edition chest

I tapped out a reply.

VIKING:

You read my mind. Give me 5 to set up

HAMMERHEAD:

K. Mics?

Hammerhead was good about giving me what I needed, and if I wasn't feeling up to talking through the mics, he never complained but happily stuck to the chat window. It was a less effective way of communicating since we had to pause what we were doing to type out a reply, but sometimes I needed the silence. I found myself needing it less and less lately, though. To my surprise, we'd clicked from the minute we'd met, and that *never* happened to me. Yet now, I counted Hammerhead among my handful of genuine friends.

We had a level of anonymity, thanks to our gaming personas, but I felt secure enough around him to share bits of information about myself in and around our conversations about the game. We hadn't gone too deep, and we hadn't shared anything personally identifiable, but he knew the basics about me, other than the fact I was studying for a minor in dance. I wasn't sure why I hadn't yet shared that particular piece of information with him. It might have had something to do with the fact that everyone always seemed surprised and confused when they found out I was studying a creative arts subject alongside a technical major. My own dad had told me several times it was "weird" for me to be studying dance, and his words had stuck in my mind.

Back to Hammerhead. I knew he was a guy, a second-year student like me, studying for a degree in engineering. Other than gaming, he played for his uni football team. He came across as a patient, easy-going guy, and sometimes I wished I could meet him in person, although I'd probably ruin it with my anxiety and lifelong habit of overthinking every single thing.

Speaking of my anxiety... While I hadn't shared my real-life struggles with Hammerhead, he'd come up with a unique way to try and push me out of my comfort zone online.

In real life, Connor and Niall were mostly about the direct route, asking me to do things outright. My dance friend JJ was like my hype man, encouraging me until I somehow believed I was capable of things I'd normally be too afraid to do. But online, I had Hammerhead, and he had a different approach to pushing me out of my comfort zone.

He dared me.

For example—the first time we'd spoken through our mics. I'd been hesitant, ridiculously nervous about crossing a boundary, but he'd made it into a dare, complete with a reward—a rare in-game armour. I'd somehow found myself stepping up, and just like that, we'd started talking and never really stopped.

Shaking myself out of my thoughts, I returned my attention to my PC monitor as I replied.

VIKING:

Yes to mics

Slipping into my online persona, where I could be a confident badass warrior—something I'd never achieve in reality—I switched on my microphone.

Shy, anxious Leo was gone...for now, and Viking was ready to play.

TWO

FINN

The bottle spun. Barely paying it any attention, I sipped from my beer bottle as I tapped out a message on my phone to Viking, confirming the start time of tonight's online campaign.

"Finn. Finn." An elbow jabbed into my side, and I raised my head to find my football teammate Pete eyeing me expectantly from my left. To my right, there was now an empty space where Ellie had been. She'd crawled across the circle and was kissing Nicola, straddling her lap. Right. It was my turn to spin.

My phone vibrated softly, and I glanced down at the screen, my lips curving upwards as I took in the words.

VIKING:

> Any chance we could start earlier tonight?
> Today has been stressful. I could do with a
> distraction

I clapped Pete on the shoulder. "All yours, bro. I'm heading out."

He shook his head at me, muttering something about

boring bastards, but I was already on my feet and making my way out of his student house.

I probably should've made more of an effort, but I'd thought we were going to just hang out and watch the football. Somehow, Pete's housemate had turned it into an impromptu games night, inviting several girls from his course, and then alcohol had become involved, and yeah, somehow, we'd ended up playing spin the bottle with an empty vodka bottle.

Fuck, I really was boring, wasn't I? Who would complain about any of that? I never would have before, but over the last four or five months, I'd become obsessed with a certain game, probably to an unhealthy level.

Ah, well. Too late to change things now. I had a date with *Lesath Legends*, and a certain Viking was waiting for me.

Settled in my gaming chair in my bedroom, I adjusted my mic as I waited for the portal to load up. Living at home with my parents and younger brother rather than paying for student accommodation meant I got to access all my home comforts, which included my PlayStation. With *Lesath Legends* introducing cross-platform support a few months earlier, it meant I got to play with and against thousands of players on different consoles and PCs all over the world. I'd stumbled across Viking the day the cross-platform play had come out of beta, and we'd hit it off straight away. Both of us seemed to end up online around the same time in the evening, and I'd eventually messaged him to ask if he wanted to partner up for a campaign.

Now, here we were, playing online together almost every night.

"Ready for this?"

Viking's voice came through the mic, confirming he was

ready to go. As usual, I couldn't help wondering what his real voice sounded like. Both of us had the in-game privacy mode enabled that distorted our voices. Maybe I'd dare him to share his real voice with me one day, but we'd only just swapped phone numbers, and that was only so we could arrange our gaming times more easily.

Back to the reason I was here and not spinning a bottle, hoping it wouldn't land on someone I didn't want to kiss. "What happened today? Why were you stressed?"

I heard Viking's breath hitch, and then there was silence. Just when I'd given up the question as a lost cause, he replied. "I was doing a project for one of my modules, and I had to do a ten-minute presentation for it today. I...I tried to prepare myself for it, but when the time came, I froze." His voice lowered. "Fucking stupid, right? I'm an adult, more than halfway through my degree course. I shouldn't be having these issues still."

The game buzzer sounded. "Ready up," I said, tapping my controller as our on-screen characters dropped into the area of the map we'd been exploring last night. Directing my character towards a dilapidated wooden building, I returned the conversation to Viking. "It's not stupid. Why did you freeze?"

"I-I-I—*fuck*," he whimpered, and I dropped my controller, swiping my phone from the bed. Fuck it. If he really didn't want to talk to me, he didn't have to answer. I hit his number and dialled, switching to speakerphone, before I picked up my controller again.

"H-hello?"

The voice was softly spoken, warm, and a little hesitant. My lips curved upwards. So this was how Viking sounded in reality. We'd never crossed this line before, but there was clearly something going on with him, and I *needed* to hear his voice. Properly.

"Hi. It's nice to hear your proper voice."

A shaky sigh came through the speaker. "Okay, I can do this," he mumbled before clearing his throat. "You sound different to how I imagined."

"Yeah?"

"Yeah. I dunno why. I imagined you with a Scouse accent for some reason. Your game voice sounds a bit Scouse, sometimes."

I chuckled, but it died away quickly when I remembered why I'd called him, and it wasn't to discuss accents. "Hey..." I began. "Want to tell me why you froze?"

"I guess so. It—it's hard to talk about. I... Ever since I was a kid, I've been...shy. And, uh, anxious, I guess. To the point where I can't speak to people without stuttering or losing my breath or going red and—and—and—"

"It's okay. You're talking to me, and it's all good. Even if any of those things happen when you're talking to me, you know I won't ever judge you, right?"

He sighed again. "Yeah, but it's easier with you. I don't have to speak to you in person. Face to face. And you, I don't know, you're easy to talk to. Maybe because there's no pressure because we're both doing an activity that relaxes me."

"I get that." Steering my character towards his, I pulled up my inventory to transfer a medipack to his character. "It's natural to be more relaxed around people who share our interests when we know they're not gonna judge us. I can't say I've ever experienced the level of discomfort it sounds like you have—I like to think I'm pretty confident on the whole—but I've been in situations well out of my comfort zone. I understand where you're coming from."

"I wish I had your confidence," he said miserably. "Here I am in my second year of uni, and the most social interaction I'm getting is gaming with you. I don't even go to student parties or anything. My housemate dragged me to the student union a couple of times, but I spent the entirety of both times feeling so uncomfortable, like I was on display and everyone was looking at me. Even though they probably weren't. I'm never gonna be able to flirt, let alone have a relationship or whatever, if I can't talk to anyone. Even if I could talk, the rest of it is beyond me. Kissing someone? I have no fucking clue where to begin. I'm a lost cause."

The words came out all in a rush, like he'd been bottling them up deep inside and needed to get them off his chest, and after a deep breath, he continued. "Connor and Niall—my two course friends—were doing the presentation with me today, and they helped me through it, but I feel fucking awful. I let them down. They did their parts just fine, and I couldn't even get through my bit without them coaching me through it."

Fuck. The despair in his voice was killing me.

"You didn't let them down. I know you, and I know that you're a good—great person, okay? There's no way they'd hold it against you."

"Oh," he whispered.

"Yeah. You froze up. So what? It's not the end of the world. I bet your lecturers are gonna be impressed with your project."

He sighed. "I hope you're right." But his voice sounded a little brighter, and I could breathe more easily.

"Hey. How about a dare? I dare you to tell me your name. We're talking on the phone with our real voices; I can't call you Viking."

"I-I guess not. Uh. I'm...um...Erik."

"With a *K*? Like Erik the Red? I guess calling you Viking wasn't too far from the truth."

"No," he said quietly.

"I'm Finn. You can blame my brother for my Hammerhead name. He used to call me 'Sharkfin' because that was a hilarious nickname to his eight-year-old brain, and not long after that, I was chasing him around the house with an inflatable hammer—don't ask—so, yeah. Hammerhead shark. I dunno. I'm no good at coming up with names."

"Finn."

I smiled. "Hi, Erik."

"Fuck," he whispered. "I'm—I need to go. Today's been — I need to sleep."

"Okay. Speak to you—" I began, but he was already gone.

THREE

FINN

"What am I doing here?" I wondered aloud as I took in my surroundings. I'd never been to this part of campus before, and this performance studio was unchartered territory for me.

"*We* are here supporting our bestie, as you well know." Ander, my LSU football teammate, cuffed me around the back of the head. I shot him a mock glare.

"Watch it. JJ's not my bestie. I barely even know the guy. He still holds a grudge because I ruined his trainers back when we were freshers."

"Yeah, so you being here now will make up for it," Ander told me with a decisive nod.

"If you say so." Maybe he was right.

JJ had sent Ander a text asking him if he'd watch his dance showcase rehearsal and bring some of the football team so the dancers could practise in front of an audience. At the time, I'd been at the student union with Ander, his boyfriend Elliot, and their housemates Charlie and Levi. Ander had basically bribed us all into coming with promises of beer, and so...here we were.

Settling into my seat, I dug my phone out of my pocket and tapped out a quick message to Erik to let him know I'd be online later. That done, I killed time browsing through my social media while I waited for the rehearsal to begin.

We didn't have to wait for long. JJ appeared on the stage, along with a cute, smiling blonde girl and a guy with tousled red hair who was staring at the floor, looking as if he'd rather be anywhere than here. JJ introduced himself and the others—Alyssa, who would be dancing first, and Leo, who would dance second. After JJ's dance, they'd finish up with a group dance, and then I'd be free to make my escape and play *Lesath Legends*.

Speaking of *Lesath Legends*, I was impatient to speak to Erik. He'd texted me about half an hour earlier, asking me to wish him luck for putting himself through something he referred to as potentially the scariest thing he'd ever had to do. He'd told me he couldn't bring himself to talk about it beforehand, but he'd give me all the details afterwards. Ever since I'd seen his message, I'd been on edge, needing to know what it was and hoping he was okay, whatever it was he was doing.

But when the lights dimmed and the spotlight came on, I temporarily forgot everything else, transfixed by the first performance. It wasn't even that Alyssa was hot and wearing tight clothing that showed off the athletic curves of her body, but it was the way she moved. Fucking incredible.

"Hey, Ander." I leaned into him after she'd disappeared off the stage. "Maybe we should bring in some dance-style warm-ups to our football practices. Some of the team could do with loosening up. Moves like that—we'd be fucking unstoppable."

Ander's brows flew up. "You just watched *her* dancing like *that*, and what you got from it was that we need to incorporate the moves into our football sessions?" He shook his head. "You're a lost cause."

"What? Why?"

"Because you were watching a hot girl with some fucking hot moves, and you're thinking about football? Yeah, I'm in a relationship, and no one will ever be as hot to me as Elliot is." He paused, spinning in his seat to press a loud kiss to Elliot's cheek before he returned his attention to me. "But I have eyes. Yours, my friend, are dysfunctional. I know you're straight because you said so last semester when that guy was trying to get your number at that pub quiz. *And* your ex-girlfriend looks a bit like Alyssa, so I know she's probably your type. So, again. You're a lost cause."

"There's a reason we split up. I was only with her for about six weeks, and it was right at the start of our first year, so it's hardly worth mentioning. And I don't really have a type, FYI."

"Wasn't she a dancer?"

"She did yoga, like, once a week."

"Athletic girls. See. My point still stands."

"Whatever. Yeah, Alyssa's hot. Maybe if I saw her out and about, I might think about it. But my whole life doesn't revolve around women, okay? I know that's an unusual concept for you, with the way you were pre-Elliot." Patting his shoulder, I smirked at him.

"For someone who's hot—and I'm qualified to say that with my status as a modern bisexual man—a footballer, and reasonably intelligent, you're wasting your talents."

"Yeah, but that's stereotyping, isn't it? Hot plus athlete equals a player with a different girl every night. Okay, some people are like that, but I never have been. I guess living with my parents has kind of made it difficult to do that anyway, but for me, gaming holds equal, if not more, importance than girls."

His jaw dropped as if I'd shared some life-changing news, but he recovered quickly, a smirk replacing his shocked expression. "Oh. You like fictional women. I get it. You want those game characters with massive tits and—"

I clamped my hand over his mouth, feeling him grin beneath my palm. "You're stereotyping again."

When I pulled my hand away, he sighed dramatically. "Such rude behaviour. I expected better from you." His gaze flicked to the front of the performance studio. "Look. Leo's up now."

I returned my attention to the stage. As the guy stepped into the spotlight, I could see his body shaking, his green eyes wide and scared. Fuck. I pushed down the automatic urge to comfort him, my brain instantly going to Erik, knowing what a hard time he had going up in front of people. From everything I knew about him, I couldn't imagine him ever being on a stage and doing something like this.

The music started up, and Leo remained frozen in place. Next to me, I heard Ander's muttered "Shit," but I kept my gaze on Leo, willing him to move. There was movement to the side of the stage, and then the spotlight dimmed, soft sidelights blinking on instead. Leo's expression changed to one of determination, and when the music started from the beginning again, he began to move.

I'd thought Alyssa was amazing, but there was something about Leo that had me caught up in his performance, making me feel weirdly emotional watching him dance, his body moving effortlessly across the stage like he was born to do it. When he finished and the final notes of music died away, I clapped harder than I ever had in my life. This guy had overcome his fear and completely smashed it.

"So?" Ander nudged me as Leo made his way off the stage. "What's the verdict?"

"Fucking incredible," I said. "The way he looked so scared at the beginning, and then he did that whole routine...yeah. Incredible."

"No comments about football this time? Are you sure you're straight?"

"For fuck's sake, Ander. What's up with you today?"

His teasing grin disappeared. "Sorry. I'm just fucking with you. I can't help it sometimes. I should probably tone it down."

"Nah, it's part of your personality. I can handle it, and you know I don't take it personally."

He gave me a fist bump, and then we settled back in our seats to watch JJ's performance. And yeah, it was easy to see that he was a star. Being a part-time paid dancer obviously helped him refine his skills, but that man was clearly talented and insanely flexible. He could bend in ways I wouldn't even want to attempt.

"Fucking amazing. Fucking bendy," I said to Ander when the dance had finished before he could ask me what I thought of the performance.

Ander nodded. "Did you know I almost beat him in a dance contest?"

I stared at him. "You were in a dance contest with JJ?"

"Yeah, at Revolve. It was a lap dance competition. I got to dance for my boyfriend—not that he was my boyfriend then, and I was in denial or whatever. The point is, I almost beat a professional dancer to the title."

"Almost." The amused voice came from his other side,

and Elliot slid his arm around Ander's shoulders. "But you were my winner."

Ander smiled softly, leaning into Elliot. He kept his gaze on me, but he squeezed his boyfriend's thigh in acknowledgement. "Yep. I came second, and it was my first-ever time giving a lap dance. Have you ever given anyone one? It's harder than it looks."

Stretching my legs out in front of me, I shook my head. "Nope. I've never even had a lap dance."

"Awww. Poor Finn. Want me to give you one now to make up for it?"

"Don't even think about it," I warned him.

Levi leaned around him and Elliot, meeting my gaze with an eye roll. "Count yourself lucky. I had to watch him and JJ practising their dance routine in my house. No fucking escape when you live with them."

"You and Asher filmed me when you were watching. Don't deny you liked it."

I missed Levi's reply to Ander. The three dancers appeared back onstage, immediately stealing my attention.

My gaze scanned them again as they began their group routine. Ander was right—Alyssa was gorgeous, and when I looked at them all together with a critical eye, they made an attractive trio. Their looks weren't important, though—it was the way they moved. Their routine was strong, and although I knew nothing about dance, to me, their moves looked as good as anything I'd seen in a music video. There was no sign of Leo's earlier nerves, which was good because it meant I could relax back in my seat and enjoy the show before I returned to reality.

My reality? *Lesath Legends* and Erik.

"Hi." I grinned at Erik's character as if he could see me. "How did your thing go? If you wanna talk about it. I saw someone earlier who reminded me of you."

"Ready up," he instructed, and the countdown began. "Hi. Yeah. I...I feel really good. Great, in fact. Who reminded you of me?"

"I was doing a favour for a uni friend earlier. My friend's housemate is a dancer, and he had this dance rehearsal thing. I think it was a kind of test performance." I broke off when we landed in the game, spinning my character in a three-hundred-and-sixty-degree circle to view our surroundings. "Wait—let's head into the swamp region this time. See if we can loot any chests."

"D-dance rehearsal?" His voice was so quiet I had to strain to hear him. His character followed mine as we jogged down a cobbled path into the mists that marked the swamp area.

"Yeah. There were three people, and they did individual dances, then a group dance at the end. There was this one guy who got on the stage, and he kind of froze. He seemed really nervous, you know? But he pushed through it, and he did a fucking amazing routine." I paused, slashing at a monster that had suddenly appeared on the path before I continued. "It just made me think of you. Y'know, with your presentation. The day we first started talking to each other. I was proud of him for going through with the dance, and I'm so fucking proud of you, Erik. And whatever you did today, I'm proud of you for that, too."

There was a sharp intake of breath from Erik. "I feel sick," he mumbled. "I-I-I'm gonna go."

The call cut off, and his character disappeared from the game.

What the fuck?

Returning to the home screen, because I couldn't play this campaign as a single player, I dropped my controller to send him a text.

ME:

Are you ok?

ERIK:

Sick. Sorry. Talk soon

ME:

Ok get some rest. I'll be here when you're ready

As I stared down at my phone, there was a knock at my open bedroom door, and my younger brother, Ed, poked his head around it. "What's that face for?"

"Nothing. I dunno. Maybe something." I threw my phone onto my bed. "I was playing with my friend, and he said he was sick and disappeared. But a couple of minutes earlier, he seemed fine. He even said he was feeling great."

"Probably sick of playing that game for the millionth time." He gave my TV a pointed glance. "You have the worst taste, bro. I feel sorry for you."

"Fuck off. I'm being serious."

Ed shrugged, crossing the room and dropping onto my bed. "People can get suddenly sick, you know. Just check up on him. It's probably a bug." Staring at me suspiciously, he added, "I don't want to catch anything. I have to meet my tutor to go through my photography project tomorrow."

"Don't worry, I haven't met up with him in person." Would I ever? I hoped so.

"Does he have any hot girl friends? Why don't you ever invite any of your hot girl friends over? What's the point of having an older brother if you can't flirt with his friends? You're on the football team. You should have, like, at least a hundred girls in your phone, and you know I like older women."

"You—" I pointed at him. "—are an incredibly annoying person."

His fake pout disappeared, and he kicked me in the shin, the little bastard. "I'm a fucking *gift*. You're incredibly lucky to have such an amazing brother."

"Not as lucky as you are to have such an amazing older sibling. To answer your question, I don't particularly want to invite a load of uni girls over and have to watch the painful sight of my sixteen-year-old brother attempting to flirt with them. Then there's the fact that most of them live in student housing while I'm still at home. It's easier for me to go to other people's houses, you know?"

"Obviously, dickhead. It'll be the same for me when I start uni. I like living here, but sometimes I feel like I'll be missing out on the full student experience. Mum and Dad are great, and we won't have to pay for accommodation or the food we eat at home. I can't complain. It's just..."

My humour died away. "Yeah. I feel the same. Listen, why don't you come to one of our football practices? There are normally girls watching us, and you'll get more of a chance to speak to whoever you want because it's a lot quieter than a match. Don't expect anything because, realistically, they're not gonna be interested because of the whole age thing, but yeah, you're always welcome."

"You mean that? You wouldn't mind if I came to watch you?" His eyes widened, and I suddenly felt like the world's worst brother because how the fuck had I managed to make my sibling feel like he wasn't welcome to watch me play?

"I'd be more than happy for you to come and watch me.

Just respect the women and back off if they're not interested, okay? And if anyone gives you trouble, let me know, and I'll kick their ass. I didn't do jujitsu for three years for nothing, you know."

"Yeah, you're a real hard man." He punched my bicep with a smirk that softened into a genuine smile. "Thanks, though. I appreciate it. And I'm not being serious about flirting with your friends...okay, you know I like older women, but I'm realistic. I'm not gonna be on their radar right now, but it can be practice for my grand opening when I'm eighteen and a uni student and I'm on equal footing with them."

"Your grand opening. Fucking hell," I muttered under my breath. "Yeah. Practice makes perfect, and you need a lot of practice," I said more loudly, ducking away from the punch that he aimed at me following my words. "Seriously, though, you're welcome. Anytime. You can come to any of my matches too, if you want. Bring your friends. I'll sort you out with tickets."

He sighed dramatically. "I guess I am lucky to have you." My phone vibrated between us, and his gaze flicked to my screen. "Hey, you have a new message."

I dived for my phone before Ed could get his hands on it, unlocking the screen, a weight I'd been holding instantly disappearing as I read the message.

ERIK:

Sorry for earlier. Feeling a bit better now.
Talk soon

He'd added a little smiley emoji at the end of the message. *He was okay.*

I turned to my brother. "Are you busy? Want me to teach you how to become a master at *Lesath Legends*?"

"You're lucky I'm bored. Give me a controller, and I'll show you how it's done."

FOUR

LEO

L ies, lies, and more lies. Why had I given Finn a fake name in the first place? Okay, I knew why, but my reasons were looking increasingly flimsy the more I thought about them. When he'd initially called me, I'd been so panicked about my real self not stacking up to my online persona I'd thrown out the first name I could think of. When I was Erik or Viking, I wasn't Leo. I could be a bit braver. I could manage to speak to my online friend on the phone like a normal person—whatever normal was. I could tell him things that Leo never could. It was like I was getting to speak to him from behind my online shield, even though we were talking on a phone with our real voices. And I knew his real name.

Somehow, it had never crossed my mind that he'd be a student at my university. The fact was, outside our online friendship, I spoke to a grand total of four people regularly and one semi-regularly—my dad, who was in Salisbury. I was in my own insular world, and the outside rarely penetrated.

Finn clearly had no idea it had been me at the rehearsal.

And why would he? I'd told him I was doing a degree in computing, but I'd never told him I was also studying for a minor in dance. When he'd brought up the fact that he'd actually been at my rehearsal and noticed me freeze up onstage, I hadn't been lying when I told him I felt sick. The nausea had been sudden and uncontrollable, and I'd spent a miserable few hours curled into a ball on my bed, breathing through waves of sickness and contemplating just how badly I'd fucked things up with the one person I'd ever connected with online. The person I thought I could call a friend, who'd probably never speak to me again when he found out the truth.

Why can't I be normal? Why can't I be like everyone else? What's wrong with me?

A tear trickled down my cheek and I angrily wiped it away. Just to torture myself some more, I picked up my phone, reading back through the group chat with JJ and Alyssa I'd had two days ago, right after the dance rehearsal.

JJ:

> So so proud of you today Leo. You pushed through the nerves and put on an amazing performance

> Alyssa! I'm so proud of you too. You were fucking incredible

ALYSSA:

> You were amazing! Both of you! I feel lucky I get to dance with you guys

ME:

> Thanks *heart emoji* I made a few mistakes. You were both perfect

JJ:

> We all made mistakes, but I can guarantee that no one watching would have noticed. You were really good Leo. Don't doubt yourself. You're a talented dancer

ALYSSA:

> I second this! Dream team *heart emoji*

Reading their messages had warmed me all over, but the warmth disappeared when I scrolled to the later messages. The ones right after my disastrous conversation with Finn. The question was burning inside me, and I *needed* to know.

ME:

> Who came to watch us dance today?

ALYSSA:

> Other than your friend Niall, there were my friends Erin and Amy. JJ's housemates Ander, Elliot, Charlie and Levi. JJ? Who was the other one?

> Wait I think JJ's out tonight so he might not see this. I can check with Erin, I know she talked to a couple of them

> I remembered his name! Finn from the football team

Finn from the football team.

There was the confirmation, right there on my screen. Finn was the person I'd been pouring my heart out to. The person who'd become my friend. It had taken another two days after finding out his name for me to crack, but now here I was, stalking him online. First, I searched for his social media accounts. It didn't take long—from JJ, I went to Ander, and there he was, in the list of people Ander was following.

Finn Carsley.

Now, I studied his photos. At first glance, he was a typical athlete type, like Ander. There were pictures of him shirtless on a beach playing football, showing his toned muscles. Laughing with his friends in a bar, his brown hair tousled and his deep blue eyes sparkling as he beamed, his defined jaw dusted with stubble. He was obviously popular, an athlete, and yes, he played *Lesath Legends* online with me, but I was easily replaceable. There were thousands of other players online, and I was sure the majority of them carried a lot less baggage than I did.

My decision was made. I pulled up my text message thread with Finn. The sooner I accepted the fact that I'd ruined everything between us with my lies, the sooner we could both move on.

Swallowing hard, I forced myself to type the words. My vision blurred, and I rubbed at my eyes with one hand as I hit Send.

ME:

I'm really sorry. I lied to you

I didn't even have a minute to catch my breath before a reply came through.

FINN:

You're here! I was worried. Are you feeling better? What did you lie about?

No, I'm feeling worse. I lied about my entire personality.

ME:

Not really better but not for the reasons you probably think. I lied about who I was and I'm sorry. I lied about being sick too

FINN:

> WTF?

My phone started buzzing in my hand, Finn's name flashing up on the screen. I couldn't do it. I swiped to decline the call, biting down on my trembling lip.

You fucking coward.

ME:

> I gave you a fake name when we exchanged names. I didn't want to be me. I couldn't be me. It's so fucking stupid but I couldn't be me and talk to you. I realised you'd seen me when you were telling me about the guy who'd frozen on the stage. That was me

There was a long, long pause while I gripped my phone in my trembling hand, my heart in my throat. I didn't even know why I was waiting for a reply. I'd sealed my fate already.

The screen lit up again.

FINN:

> Fuck. I don't even know what to say. That was you?

ME:

> Yeah. I understand why you won't want to speak to me again. For what it's worth, you've been a really good friend to me. I hope you have a great life

Switching my phone off, I rolled over and buried my face in my pillow.

A banging sound had me blinking my eyes open, disorientated for a second before it all came back to me.

Finn. My confession. The loss of a friend.

It hurt so fucking much, and it was all my fault.

Pulling myself into a seated position, I rubbed at my swollen eyes. The banging sounded again.

"Not now, Connor," I croaked.

My bedroom door flew open, and my stomach went into free fall. It wasn't my housemate standing there.

"No," Finn said, stalking straight into my room like he had every right to be there, a dark look on his face that was such a contrast to the smiling, playful faces he made in his photos, my breath caught in my throat. "You've been a really good friend to me? Have a great fucking life?"

I shrank back on the bed, completely lost. What was I supposed to do? Was he really here in the flesh, not just as a picture through my phone or a voice in my ear?

He noticed my reaction, and his expression softened slightly, although there was still a hard set to his jaw. "Leo Evans. You don't want to know how many hours it took me to find out where you were. But I didn't stop, and do you know why? Because you're my fucking friend, and you don't get to decide that our friendship is over because of one tiny mistake."

"I-it wasn't a tiny mistake," I whispered. "I gave you a fake name. I wanted... When I was online, I-I liked that I could be someone else. That I didn't have to be Leo, the person who fucks up all the time and can't even get through a fucking presentation or dance rehearsal without it becoming a-a major crisis."

"Fucking hell," he muttered, rubbing his hand over his jaw. "Have you been lying to me about anything else? Whenever we've been talking?"

Shaking my head, I dug my fingernails into my palm. "N-no."

"Then it's just your name. And I get why you'd do that. I know you. Viking, Erik, Leo. They're all *you*. We've been getting to know each other for a while now, and as I just said, I know you. I like to think I'm a good judge of character, and I like you. You're my friend."

"B-but I—"

"Stop." Lowering himself into a crouch, he reached out, steadying himself on the side of my bed with one hand, the other outstretched towards me. "I'm gonna tell you right now that you're overreacting, and I don't want you to give yourself a hard time about it, okay?" He studied me intently, and gradually, the hardness faded from his expression. His lips curved into a small smile. "Don't look so worried. Let's start again. Hi, I'm Finn."

Swallowing hard, I shifted forwards, wrapping my fingers around his and letting him shake my hand. "H-hi. I'm Leo."

He released my hand, and I tried not to wince, thinking about just how sweaty my palms were. Glancing around the room, his gaze landed on my PC, and his smile grew. "Want to play *Lesath Legends*?"

I could barely speak past the giant fucking lump in my throat. How had he accepted what I'd done that easily? I nodded, blinking rapidly.

"Fucking hell. C'mere," he muttered, and the next thing I knew, he was yanking me into what might have been the most awkward hug of my life. When he released me, he was biting down on his lip. "Sorry. Uh...my family is all about the hugs, and you looked like you needed one."

What was happening? I stared down at my hands. "I-I didn't mind."

Because I was still intently studying my hands, I didn't see his expression, but I heard the smile in his voice. "Honestly, Leo. Forget about what happened. It's all good. Let's play, and I can show you the cave I found yesterday. There's a chest in there we can loot if we can take out the guards."

"Yeah?"

"Yeah."

"Okay."

And just like that, it was really okay, and I had no idea how or why. Finn sat at my desk while I sat on the bed, and we played a split-screen version of our game. The weird thing was that it wasn't weird at all. There was none of the shyness and anxiety I felt around other people other than my four friends. Somehow, I found myself able to speak to him like I always had done, right from the beginning. It was easier now he wasn't looking at me, of course, and that our conversation was mostly based around the game.

"So," he said eventually when we'd cleared the cave of guards and looted the chest. "You know how I dared you before to talk to me on the phone? I have an idea for another dare, if you're interested."

"A dare?" I finally looked at him, and there was a hesitance in his gaze, but he nodded firmly. I thought about it for a minute. This was Finn, the friend who'd somehow instantly forgiven me for what I'd done and was still treating me like he normally did. "Okay...what's the dare?"

"I dare you to let me help you with your confidence. Like, if you want, I dunno, help with any situations that you know are gonna make you feel nervous, like your presentation or performance. I could, uh, I could help you prepare for them or something."

"How would that work as a dare?"

He shrugged. "We can play it by ear. Individual dares

for each thing. I'll come up with some ideas. What do you say?"

I'd been given a second chance, and if Finn was patient enough to help me with the shyness that could be debilitating at times, then I'd be a fool not to take him up on his offer.

Raising my eyes to his, I spoke, pushing through my natural urge to drop my gaze, feeling my cheeks flushing but not caring for once. "I'd like that. I need all the help I can get. But what are you getting out of it? If there's anything you want in return, say so, and if I can do it, I will."

He shot me a crooked grin. "Helping you to find your confidence is reward enough. Like I already said, you're my friend, and if I can make your life a bit easier, I will. But hey, if I need a PC expert or someone to teach me dance moves, I know where to go. Ander couldn't believe I'd never had a lap dance—" Cutting himself off, he smacked his hand over his mouth, and this time, he was the one with flushed cheeks. "Fuck's sake. I didn't mean anything by that. It was just a stupid comment. I'm not trying to get you to give me a lap dance or anything."

"Um. Good." A nervous laugh fell from my throat. "I haven't, either. Had one. Or g-given one." The thought was laughable. I couldn't imagine *ever* having that level of confidence, not even close.

"Uh, how about we stop talking about lap dances?"

"*Please.*" We looked at each other, and both laughed. Finn shook his head.

"Why am I the one getting flustered here? I'm meant to be the guru. The Jedi Master or whatever."

"Does that make me your apprentice?"

"Yeah. I guess it does."

FIVE

FINN

I dipped my head to Leo's ear, speaking low so my parents and brother didn't overhear. "I dare you to get up on that stage tomorrow and—okay, this is gonna sound really cliché—dance like no one's watching. There's a reward in it for you. A good one." I knew this was a huge deal for him—his biggest challenge so far when it came to performing in front of people—so I'd do anything I could do to help him along the way.

His head shot around to mine. "How did you know I was worrying?"

"Because I know you." I grinned at him. "You're gonna smash it. I know you are."

"Boys! Dinner's ready." My dad cleared his throat loudly, and I grabbed Leo's wrist, tugging him towards the kitchen table. Ever since the whole name incident, it felt as if he'd dropped the final barriers between us, bringing us even closer, and it hadn't taken me long to invite him over to mine—initially as a dare. My parents had fallen in love with him instantly, and even my brother seemed to like him, keeping his natural dickishness to a minimum after a well-timed threat to his life from me. The weird thing? For someone who had shyly confessed that he only had four friends—five when you included me—Leo had taken to my family like he'd been in our lives for years, not just a matter of weeks. Maybe it was different because my parents basically treated him like another son. Who knew? The point was Leo was happy to be around them, and therefore, I was happy.

"This looks great." Leo gave my mum a shy smile as she passed him with a dish of green beans. Placing the dish in the centre of the table, she squeezed his shoulder, ruffling his hair like she did with me.

"Thank you, but I'm afraid I can't take the credit for this one. John cooked today."

My dad lifted his hand in acknowledgement, continuing to dish out grilled chicken breasts to everyone. "It's your dance showcase tomorrow, Leo, and we wanted to make sure we were feeding you something appropriate before the big day. Protein is what you need."

"Yeah, me too. Gotta build up my muscles." Ed flexed his non-existent biceps, and I snorted.

"What muscles? Mum, do you have a magnifying glass so I can see what he's talking about?"

"Be nice to your brother," she said with an eye roll. Glancing over at Leo, I saw him smiling to himself, and that warmed me all over. He hadn't gone into a lot of detail about his home life, but I knew his mum had died when he was only a baby, and he wasn't all that close to his dad. He was an only child, too. Or had been until my family had basically adopted him.

"Leo, back me up. My biceps are bigger than they were last week, aren't they?"

"Um." Leo sucked his bottom lip between his teeth,

biting back his smile as he pretended to study Ed's arms. "Yeah, I'd say so."

"Thank you!" Ed shouted, fist pumping the air. "Fuck you, Sharkfin!"

"No swearing at the table," my dad bellowed. "That includes rude gestures," he added when I subtly gave Ed the middle finger. "Sorry, Leo. You're surrounded by heathens."

Leo glanced from me to my brother and then to my dad. "A-at least I get to go home at the end of the day. You have to live with them."

A wide smile spread across my face. The fact he was comfortable enough to join in my family's teasing...

"Ha!" My mum took her seat. "Exactly! At least someone recognises the sacrifices we make." She held up her hand to my dad for a high five.

My parents were so weird.

I pointedly cleared my throat, and my dad smirked at me. Thankfully, he seemed to remember what we were actually here for. "Okay, enough of that. Dig in, everyone. Leo needs his strength for tomorrow."

Tonight was the night Leo had been working towards for a long time, putting as much effort into it as he did with his computing projects. This showcase was the culmination of his dance module, and he was going to be judged on both his group dance and his individual one. As I made my way towards the LSU theatre along with my family, I sent him a quick text.

ME:

You'll smash this. Remember our dare.
YOU CAN DO IT

I had a read receipt but no reply, which I expected. He'd been so stressed, but I had faith in him. He could do this.

The theatre was packed with families and friends of the dancers who were performing tonight. Some of my teammates were here at the theatre, but I'd chosen to sit with my family a few rows from the front. I shifted in my seat, my own nerves getting the better of me as we drew closer to Leo's first performance.

"Bro's up next," Ed hissed, jabbing his finger at the programme, as if I hadn't been studying it intently. I nodded in acknowledgement, returning my attention to the stage.

When the lights dimmed, I found myself holding my breath, my heart rate picking up, but I didn't need to worry. Illuminated by sweeping lights, JJ, Alyssa, and Leo nailed their routine as if they'd been performing it for years, even more polished than the first time I'd seen them.

On my feet clapping and cheering, so proud of Leo—of all three of them—it took me a second to register Ed clasping my arm. "Bro. *Bro*. Leo's fucking good, isn't he?"

"Yeah." It was all I could manage to say, sinking back into my chair as the stage darkened again. He'd been amazing, and now all he needed to do was to get through his solo performance.

My mind flashed back to his rehearsal, when I hadn't known it was him, and he'd frozen onstage. This time, it would be different. I was sure of it.

A single spotlight illuminated my friend as the opening notes of "Hard Sometimes" by Ruel sounded. I willed him to hold his nerve, to complete our dare and dance like no one was watching him.

He did it.

Effortlessly.

I was on my feet the second the final note sounded, my family right there along with me.

"Leo!" My mum pulled my friend into a hug, and then my dad was there to take her place, complete with back slapping.

"Broooo. What the fuck? Where were you hiding that talent?" Ed pushed in between them, wide-eyed...with his phone camera on, recording everything.

"Ed!" I twisted my body so it was in between his phone and Leo, who was staring at my brother with a horrified expression.

"Sorry. It's not for public consumption, don't worry." Ed waved his phone at Leo, and Leo relaxed a little. I took the opportunity to throw my arms around him, buzzing with euphoria at what he'd just achieved.

"You were amazing."

He hugged me back tentatively. "Really?"

"Really. Seriously. You were so fucking good, Leo."

"He's right, and you know I don't agree with my brother very often," Ed interjected, throwing his arms around us both. "Family hugs! Mum! Dad! Look! I'm such a nice, supportive brother, aren't I?"

"You're such a dickhead, you mean," I muttered, but I didn't mean it. Ed just laughed, and Leo's grip on me went from tentative to firm, a huff of laughter sounding in my ear.

When the two of us were walking back across campus

towards Leo's student flat, my parents and brother having gone home, I spoke again.

"You really were amazing today. I hope you know that."

"I— Yeah. No. I feel...proud that I managed to do that."

"You should be." I glanced over at him with a grin. "Don't tell JJ, but I liked your dance the best."

"You're biased," he shot back, ducking his head as he shoved his hands in his pockets. I could see the pleased smile on his face that he was trying to hide.

"Maybe, but it's still true." We reached his building, and I glanced upwards. "Ready for your reward? This isn't gonna be a thing normally, but I know how much of a big deal this was for you, and...yeah...my family wanted to chip in and get you something anyway, and my mum was worried that she'd already missed your birthday and all that...so I kinda combined it all... Don't worry, I didn't tell them about our dares or anything else, but I thought—"

Leo placed a hand on my arm, cutting off my ramble. "I can't believe I'm the one saying this, but...Finn. Breathe."

"Yeah. Okay." I breathed.

We made it up to his flat, and I was on edge again, waiting for him to see my surprise. Was it weird for friends to do this for one another? No. Surely not. My family was involved, anyway, and now I knew Leo, I knew exactly how far he'd pushed himself tonight. Not just physically but mentally. He'd crossed a *huge* barrier, and I was so fucking proud of my friend. He deserved everything.

As I steered Leo towards his bedroom, I silently thanked his flatmate, Connor, for getting this set up while we were at the showcase.

Leo stopped dead in the doorway.

"What the *fuck*? Is that...?" he whispered.

"...A *Lesath Legends*-themed Secretlab gaming chair?" I finished.

His gaze flew to mine, his eyes wide. "What? How? It's *mine*?"

"Yeah, it's yours. I told you. It's your reward and also a gift from my family. Oh, Connor installed it all, too."

"This is too much. I can't accept this."

"You can. It was on sale anyway, and I can't return it." Technically, I *could*, but I wasn't going to.

"I-I don't know what to say." Stroking his hand over the top of the chair, he spun it around, staring at it with huge green eyes.

I gently gripped his shoulders, manoeuvring him so I could push him down onto the chair. My smile was so wide it made my face ache. "Don't say anything. Let's play."

SIX

LEO

"Let me get this straight. Finn, aka the shoe ruiner, has been daring you to do things for months now, and it's helping you to gain confidence? And I'm only just finding out about it now?" JJ arched a brow at me.

"Well...kind of? Not exactly. He knows about my, y'know, shyness, and...yeah, he dares me to do something about it. Okay, here's an example. The dance showcase a few weeks ago. He dared me to go out there and just dance like no one was watching me. It sounds weird, but it worked. I kept his words in mind, and I just...danced."

"Hey, if it works." JJ smiled briefly, but then his brows pulled together. "What's in it for him?"

Good question. I genuinely believed Finn had no ulterior motives, though. What would he have to gain?

"Nothing. I mean, I told him I'd help him out if he needed anything to do with computing, or dance help, or whatever, but he's doing it because he's nice?" It wasn't supposed to come out like a question, but it had the unintended effect of chasing away JJ's suspicion.

He gave an exaggerated sigh as we approached the

training pitch. "I suppose that means I'll have to forgive him for ruining my shoes. The sacrifices I make." Shaking his head, he continued before I could say anything. "Don't give me that look. I'm joking, I promise. Seriously, babe, if this is working for you, keep it up. You know I'm here for you, whatever happens. Even if I'm not with you in person, you know you can text or call me anytime."

"I know. Thank you." I glanced over at my friend, feeling a rush of warmth. "I never said thank you. Before. That day we first met at the uni open day, when you told me there was nothing stopping me from adding a dance module to my degree course."

A wide smile spread across his face. "All you needed was a little push. You had it in you. You just had to believe in yourself." Surprising me, he slung his arm around my shoulders. "Do that today, and you'll be fine. I'll be here."

"I can do this." I nodded decisively and then repeated my words in an attempt to convince myself. I'd danced in front of a packed auditorium, so why was the thought of potentially meeting some of Finn's teammates so nerve-racking? Fucking hell, I was a mess.

We took seats on the benches at the side of the training pitch, sliding in next to Niccolò, who I guessed was there to watch his boyfriend, Bennett, who was on Finn's engineering degree course. Finn had coached me on all the team members and any significant others who might be hanging around the pitch, so I had a general idea of who everyone was. Finn thought it would help me to feel more at ease if I at least knew them by sight, and I'd met Niccolò several times in passing, thanks to the fact he was JJ's best friend.

JJ himself wasn't involved with anyone on the team, other than having two footballers as housemates, but he'd come with me for moral support. I secretly hoped his boyfriend wouldn't show up today. That man was scary. Not to mention, he was one of the LSU lecturers. But JJ had heart eyes every time Dr. Wilder was around him, and it was clear how much they loved each other, so I didn't begrudge him his happiness. If anyone deserved it, it was JJ. My usual strategy was to find something urgent to do far away whenever Dr. Wilder appeared in my vicinity.

"Hi, JJ. Hi...JJ's friend. I don't think we've met."

My eyes widened at the soft, curious voice coming from the formerly empty space to my right. I turned in slow motion, as if I could delay the inevitable. I could already feel my face heating, and I cursed internally.

"H-h-hi," I managed, taking in golden-brown hair in a long, swinging ponytail and a bright smile before I lowered my gaze to my hands.

My hands...which were shaking.

I breathed out, sliding them under my thighs so they wouldn't betray me. The girl who'd taken a seat next to me didn't seem to notice anything wrong because she kept talking.

"I haven't seen you here before. Who are you here to watch? I'm Sophie. First-year photography student. My older brother Nate's on the team, but between you and me, I'm here to watch Charlie. Do you know him? He's not on the team, but he's training with them for one of his uni modules, isn't that interesting?" she rushed out. "Oh, these are my friends and course mates, Daisy and Millie. Daisy's brother Pete's also on the team, and Millie's here to watch cute footballers." She laughed, and I swallowed hard. On my left, JJ pressed his thigh against mine in a deliberate movement, reminding me he was here, and I gathered my courage. Or whatever passed for courage.

"I-I'm Leo. Um. I'm in my second year. Com—computing. I'm here for Finn. It—it's my first time here."

"Oh, Finn! Friend or boyfriend?"

My gaze flew to hers, finding only a friendly curiosity there. Boyfriend? Where would she get that idea from? Then again, this team *did* seem to have an unusually high proportion of players with boyfriends, so I guessed it was a probable conclusion. Probable, but completely incorrect.

"Friend. W-we play games online." As soon as I said the words, the colour drained from my face. Panicked thoughts whirled through my mind. Why had I said that? Was I supposed to come across as cool? Was Finn keeping his gaming a secret? Fuck, had I messed things up for him?

"You do? What do you play?" Millie leaned around Sophie. "I play *Lesath Legends* sometimes, and so does Daisy. Sophie even joins us occasionally, although she prefers *The Sims*."

"You play *Lesath Legends*?" For once in my life, my shock pushed aside my shyness. These girls were gamers?

"Don't get her started on the hot vampire character." Sophie rolled her eyes, although she was smiling. "Tell you what. I'll just switch seats with Millie, and she can tell you all about it."

Oh, fuck. No. I wasn't ready to have an actual conversation. Before I could, I dunno, run away and hide behind the nearest building, Sophie was rising to her feet, and Millie was sliding along the bench into her vacated space. I could feel my heart rate picking up, and I was struggling for breath.

Why am I like this? Please, please don't freeze up, I begged myself.

"Leo! You came."

The breath whooshed from my lungs at the sound of the

warm voice. I looked up to see a slightly out-of-breath Finn clad in his blue LSU football kit, studying me with concern in his eyes, although he had a smile on his face.

"Did you run here?"

"Yeah." He shrugged. "Saw you sitting over here, and I thought I'd come and say hi." His eyes were radiating everything he wasn't saying aloud, and I'd never felt more lucky in that moment to have a friend who instinctively understood me the way he did.

Thank you, I mouthed, and he grinned at me, relaxing.

A delicate cough sounded next to me. "Hi, Finn. I'm Millie, and you probably already know Daisy and Sophie. Leo was just telling us that the two of you play *Lesath Legends*. Me and Daisy play, too. We should arrange a quad campaign."

Finn's brows rose as he stared at me before he finally tore his gaze away, turning his attention to Millie and Daisy. From the appreciative look on his face, he liked what he saw. I could see why, although I was sure he was appreciating them in a whole different way to me. Attraction seemed to work differently for me than it did for the other people I knew. As in, I didn't feel it. I knew what it was *supposed* to feel like, but I hadn't personally experienced it. Or at least not properly. There was a girl at school I'd been friends with for a while, and I started to feel something for her—I wasn't sure exactly how to describe it, but there was something there that wasn't there with anyone else. It never went anywhere, though. She got a boyfriend, and we ended up drifting apart.

But back to Finn and the girls. Finn was now giving Daisy a flirty smile, and I knew even before he opened his mouth that Millie's suggestion was going to happen.

Except he glanced back at me, a question in his eyes. I

gave him a tiny nod. I needed to push myself, and this seemed like a good opportunity. It was *Lesath Legends*, after all.

"Yeah, sounds good. We'll be online later, if you're around. Want my number? You can text me your usernames, and we'll add you when we get back to mine."

"Yes, please." Daisy whipped her phone out of her bag, thrusting it into his hand. As he was inputting his number, a whistle blew from the other side of the pitch, and he swung around before spinning back to her.

"Gotta go. Leo and I have plans after practice, but we'll speak to you online later. Sophie, nice to see you again. I'll tell Charlie you said hi." He shot Sophie a smirk as he handed the phone back to Daisy, and she laughed as he jogged away to join his teammates and manager.

I settled back to watch the team while the girls talked among themselves in low voices, gesturing towards the players on the pitch every now and then. Once I'd worked out the identities of everyone from the research Finn had made me do, my focus returned to my friend. He looked completely at home, going through the drills with ease, glancing over at me intermittently and shooting me a quick grin every time I caught his eye.

The team lined up close to us, ready to do cone drills. Millie cleared her throat, leaning into me, the scent of something citrusy hitting my nose. "The guy that's up first? That's Nate, Sophie's brother. He's in his final year of uni. The guy behind him is Charlie, although I guess you know that already? I think he's got a bit of a thing for Sophie. They've been flirting, anyway. Not sure how her brother's gonna take it, but—"

"I can hear you, you know. Stop gossiping about me. My brother doesn't get to decide who I do and don't see, either.

Not that he'd have a problem, *if* I liked Charlie, which I'm neither confirming nor denying." Sophie shook her head in mock disappointment. "Terrible gossips, these girls. Whatever they say about me, it's all lies."

"As if we'd gossip about our queen," Daisy interjected.

"Guys, please stop with the queen thing. That whole prom king and queen thing was ridiculous." Sophie tossed her ponytail over her shoulder, huffing. She turned to me. "They're calling me that because we all went to the same school, and in sixth form, I somehow ended up as prom queen. Probably because these two put my name up for it, and no one else could be bothered to campaign. They still haven't let me forget it."

"And we never will." The girls smirked at each other, and a little of my tension disappeared because it didn't seem as if they expected me to reply. I studied Sophie's brother as they began talking among themselves once again. Tall, dark hair, tanned, he was yet another one of those effortlessly cool, confident guys that I longed to be like.

No. *Had* longed to be like. I had to keep reminding myself that one day, I'd be comfortable in my own skin.

One day. I hoped.

"Proud of you," JJ murmured, too low for the girls to hear.

"Thanks." I knocked my shoulder against his, and he smiled.

"Crisp?" Finn shoved the bag at me, dropping a handful of salt-and-vinegar Chipsticks into his mouth.

Pulling my own handful of crisps from the bag, I

nodded towards my empty glass. "I'm gonna need another drink if you keep feeding me all these salty snacks."

"Already on it. Look at what's next to my desk. See? I borrowed my dad's electric cool box and filled it up. There's bottled water, soft drinks, beer, and a couple of energy drinks if we wanna stay up late gaming."

"You thought of everything," I said, glancing around at our setup. Finn's console was on and ready to go, with our controllers and headsets fully charged and connected. There was a rotating fan blowing across us, keeping us cool despite the warm breeze coming through the open window, and the bed was piled high with pillows and cushions and blankets.

The only thing left to do was to log in to the game.

Where I'd have to make conversation. Fuck.

Placing the crisp bag down, I rubbed my sweaty palms against my shorts.

"Leoooo." Finn rolled onto his stomach, looking up at me through his lashes. "Stop worrying. It's gonna be okay. It's just talking online. We've done this with other people when we've played quad campaigns."

"I know, but it's different because I know who they are. And I think...they were probably being friendly, but I'm pretty sure Millie smiled at me in the same way Daisy smiled at you, and she was definitely flirting with you. And I—"

He pushed himself up, lunging forwards to place his palm over my mouth. "Stop that. There's no pressure, okay? We'll play a couple of games, and we're gonna have a good time. I promise."

"Okay," I said. It came out muffled against his hand.

"Good boy." Removing his palm, he ruffled my hair, and I glared at him, which made him grin harder.

"Don't call me that."

"Sorry, little lion."

I smacked his bare calf. "No."

"Your name literally means lion." Shifting to sit against the wall next to me, he nudged his shoulder against mine. "I like that we can act like this around each other. You're fun to be around, you know."

My jaw dropped. "I am?"

"Yeah. Don't sound so surprised. I like hanging out with you."

"Oh. Uh. I like hanging out with you, too." My stupid fucking face was heating again, and I leaned forwards, hoping the fan would cool it off.

"Good." Reaching for the controllers and headsets, he held them up. "Blue or camo?"

"Blue, please."

He passed me the blue controller, and I settled my headset over my ears. Next to me, he did the same, and then our full focus turned to the game.

Finn's character rapidly descended a rocky wall, and I angled my left thumbstick, sending my character scrambling after his. He laughed aloud as I misjudged the distance and slipped, my character landing at the bottom in a heap, knocking out a huge percentage of my health bar. "Want one of my medipacks? I dare you to invite Millie for a coffee when the girls join the game."

"What? I can't do that!"

"Yeah, you can. You haven't backed out on a dare yet, and you know I'd never dare you to do something I didn't think you were capable of."

My palms were clammy around my controller at the thought of inviting someone out for coffee. Anyone who wasn't one of my handful of friends. And a girl who might have been flirting with me?

"Finn. I don't think—"

He paused the game, taking one hand off the controller, turning my head to his with a light grip on my jaw. "Yes, you can."

I studied him, noting the way his brows were pulled together, his eyes dark and serious. "Why is this so important to you?"

"Because you're my friend, and I want you to be happy. Everything we've been doing has been good, right?"

"Well, yeah." If it hadn't been for him and JJ both pushing me out of my comfort zone, I'd—I didn't even want to think about it. I'd probably be hiding away in my room, on my way to becoming a hermit. Honestly, the thought still sounded appealing. But Finn was right. I sighed. "Can we amend the dare? I— We'll play for a while, and if I feel comfortable enough, I'll do it. But you have to come, okay? You and her friend."

A wide smile stretched across his face, warming me all over. Dropping his grip on my jaw, he wrapped his arm around my back, pulling me into a hug, and after a moment's hesitation, I hugged him back.

"I wouldn't leave you, Leo. Not until you were ready. I wouldn't do that to you," he murmured before releasing me, shifting back into his original position. "Ready to play? I wanna get this bit done before the girls join us."

"Yes." I turned back to the screen, still warm all over and with a smile tugging at my lips. My smile grew bigger when he opened his inventory and handed my character a medipack, restoring my health bar.

I was still scared, light years away from the lion he'd called me earlier, but maybe I could do this.

"I-I could probably help you." Gripping the controller more tightly to mask the tremor in my hands, I forced the words out. "I've, uh, studied web design."

In my peripheral vision, I saw Finn's head whip around, and I glanced over at him. *Do it*, he mouthed.

"Really? I only need something simple to show my photos, but I haven't got a clue where to start. If you don't mind pointing me in the right direction, that would be great," Millie was saying, and I sucked in a breath. This was the moment of truth. We'd already played through two campaigns. It was getting late, and if I didn't take the chance now, it might not come up again.

"We could meet at the library. I could, uh, look at your computer." I shot Finn a pleading look that he noticed, even with his attention on the screen.

"Why not make it a group study session?" he suggested casually. "Daisy, you up for it? We could even get Charlie and Sophie to join."

"Great idea!" she said instantly. "Tuesday afternoon? Or do you guys have lectures?"

Finn was the one to answer her. "We can do 4:00 p.m. if that works?"

"Perfect. Top floor, by the windows?"

He agreed for us both, and I was distantly aware of him wrapping things up while I leaned back against the wall, my head pounding and my heart racing.

"Leo. Hey. Leo."

I blinked, refocusing on Finn's concerned face filling my vision. He carefully lifted my headset off my head and tugged my controller from my unresisting grip, and after placing them down, he was back, cradling my head with his palms as he leaned in to rest his forehead against mine.

"Hey. You're all good. It's all good. You did it."

I breathed out. "Yeah." How was I such a fuck-up that I was stressing so much about something that would be so minor to anyone else?

"I was right. You are a little lion. I'm proud of you." His thumb stroked across my cheek, and then he released me, clearing his throat as he slid off the bed. I caught a glimpse of a flush on his face.

"Are you okay?"

His gaze flew back to mine, his eyes wide. "Yeah. I—uh, it's warm in here, isn't it?" Diving for the cool box, he fished out a can of Sprite, rolling it across his cheeks.

"Maybe a bit. Blow the fan on you," I suggested, and he nodded, turning away from me to angle the fan towards him. Staring at his broad back, I bit down on my lip, thinking hard. "Finn. Can I dare you to do something?"

His shoulders stiffened, my question clearly taking him by surprise, and I rushed to continue.

"It feels like it's a bit uneven sometimes, that's all. You dare me to do all these things, constantly trying to help me, getting me out of my comfort zone, and I don't do anything for you in return."

"It's not a fucking transactional relationship," he mumbled. "You're my friend. I wanna help you out, you know this. I don't expect anything in return. Anyway, you give me plenty. You're fun to be around. I already told you that. I—fuck. I really like hanging out with you, okay?"

"Finn. Please look at me."

When he finally turned around, his face was unreadable, but there was still a flush of colour high on his cheekbones. I decided to try a tactic I'd seen my housemate Connor employ that I'd never tried before.

Scooting forwards to the edge of the bed, I gave him what I hoped was a challenging look. "Don't tell me you're too scared to accept a dare from me."

His brows flew up, interest sparking in his gaze, and encouraged, I continued.

"One little dare."

He blew out a breath, scrubbing his hand across his face, and then he rose to his feet. Crossing the room, he leaned down and placed his arms on the bed on either side of me. "Go on, then. Dare me."

I licked my lips, my nerves returning, but I'd had a lot of practice at pushing them down when it was just me and Finn, and so I held his gaze. "I dare you to let me teach you a dance routine and then for you to perform it in front of people."

His mouth dropped open, and he twisted his body sideways, letting himself fall back onto the bed next to me, his body bouncing as he hit the mattress springs. "Fucking hell. I was not expecting that dare."

"What were you expecting?" I asked curiously, flopping down next to him on my back, both of us staring up at the ceiling.

"I...uh. I dunno. Not that."

"Are you going to accept the dare?"

Rolling onto his side, he lifted himself onto his elbow. His expression turned mischievous as he held up two fingers and then tapped them against my bicep. "That was two dares. Learn the dance, then perform it. I know this isn't transactional, but maybe you should let me dare you to do something in return."

"Wasn't what I did earlier enough?" I raised my hand

and began ticking off points on my fingers. "I played two whole campaigns and made conversation. I invited Millie to meet up with us. And I still have to go through the actual meetup. I have no fucking clue how to flirt."

His fingers closed around mine, lowering my hand. He squeezed it briefly and then let go, letting out a loud, dramatic sigh.

"Fine. I guess I owe you one."

"Our relationship isn't transactional," I reminded him, earning me a light punch to my shoulder. "Seriously, though. Can you help me be less of a fuck-up? Give me some flirting pointers or whatever?"

"Yeah..." he said slowly. "If that's what you want to do."

"It is."

"Okay, then. Tomorrow night. Meet me outside the student union."

SEVEN

LEO

"See that guy over there?" Finn leaned in, his breath skating across my skin as he lowered his head to my ear. "The one with the Raiders cap?"

I followed his gaze. Directly in front of us was a guy in a baseball cap casually resting one elbow on the bar counter. His body was angled towards the girl next to him, perched on a bar stool, and he was saying something to her with a flirty grin on his face, making her smile in return.

"Look at his body language and then her body language. See how they're open to each other? Leaning in? Honestly, half of flirting—for me, at least—is checking on the other person's body language. If their posture's all stiff or they don't wanna look at you or whatever, I know there's no point in taking it any further."

"What if they're just uncomfortable to begin with, though? Like I was with you?" I shifted on my feet. My intention was to turn so I could see his face, but I ended up with the back of my left shoulder pressed against his chest. I went to take a step away, but he reached out and gripped my waist, holding me in place.

"You were never uncomfortable with me, though, were you?" His voice was so low in my ear. "Not even when you found out that I knew who you were."

"I-I guess it's different with us. We're not trying to flirt with each other, and we got to know each other online first. We were already friends."

"Yeah." He sighed against me before releasing his grip on my waist. I felt suddenly cold without his body heat to warm me. "So...watch the people around us...maybe listen in if we can get close enough, and we can discuss their techniques."

"Okay."

We spent the next hour roaming the student union, eavesdropping on conversations while trying not to seem obvious. Eventually, though, I had enough. It was clear to me from the actions we'd witnessed that I'd never be a natural flirt. I couldn't even talk to anyone normally, let alone anything more. Finn's advice was to just be myself and be friendly and listen to whoever I was speaking to rather than try to hold the conversation. It sounded simple, so why did I find it so hard?

"I'm done. Can we leave?" I said after our fifth circuit of the bar area. Finn glanced at me, a thoughtful expression on his face.

"What about a dare? I dare you to speak to one person. Not even flirt with them. Just speak. Then we'll go."

"Fiinnnn."

"Leoooo."

"Fine. But you'd better be there with me."

"Course I will be. C'mon, little lion. Let's go find someone." He grinned and slung his arm around me, pulling me into a side hug. I was beginning to get used to how tactile he was. It would've been weird with anyone else, but with

Finn, it felt normal, somehow. Nice. It reminded me of the way JJ and his friends were with each other.

We reached the room with the pool tables, and I smiled when I saw Charlie with Bennett, Levi, and Pete from the football team, playing a doubles game. Finn's dare hadn't specified who I had to speak to. Most of these guys were his teammates, and that fact should theoretically make it easier to speak to one of them.

Charlie was closest to us, chalking up the end of his cue while he watched Bennett taking a shot. He looked up when he saw us, greeting Finn with a lift of his hand and then giving me a polite smile.

Okay. I could do this. Licking my dry lips, I returned his smile with a hesitant one of my own. "H-hi. I'm Leo. Finn's friend."

He nodded. "Yeah. Hi. I saw you at that football practice with Sophie."

"Oh. Uh, I wasn't with her. Just sitting with her." My stupid fucking face was heating again. I could feel it.

"Alright, bro?" Finn took over the conversation, giving Charlie a fist bump before dragging me around to be introduced to the others.

They made small talk for a few minutes, mostly about football, but Finn stuck to my side, glancing over at me every now and then as if he wanted to make sure I was doing okay. I appreciated him doing so, but I...I'd done it. I'd introduced myself to someone new, and it hadn't been anywhere near as bad as I'd been building it up in my head. I had the feeling that a lot of my issues were due to my brain running wild and making me think things that weren't true.

"We'll catch up with you later. We've got an important date with *Lesath Legends*," Finn announced to the four of them when there was a break in the conversation. Lifting his hand in a wave, he backed away from the pool table. I followed his lead, giving a tiny wave of my own and receiving matching grins from them.

When I turned back to Finn, I found him watching me with a look I could only describe as fond. As we left the building, he pulled me into him again, ruffling my hair.

"I'm so fucking proud of you."

"Thanks. I'm proud of me, too." I was. It was such a small thing to most people, but it was a big deal to me.

Without even discussing it, we both headed back to Finn's house, where his dad greeted us with warm hugs. "Evening, lads. Let me guess—gaming?"

"Always." Finn opened the fridge, scanning the contents. "What do you want to drink, Leo? Beer? Coke? Juice?"

"Pass me a beer," his dad said, holding out his hand expectantly.

"What am I, your waiter?" Finn tutted as he handed his dad the beer. His dad cuffed him around the head playfully.

"Less of your cheek, please. Follow Leo's example. He's the only one with manners out of the two of you." He winked at me, and I felt a grin spread across my face.

"He's right. You need to learn some manners," I told Finn, and both he and his dad laughed. When we'd escaped to his room, beers in hand, he nudged me with his shoulder.

"You realise that you're the favourite son now?"

"Maybe you should practise being more like me."

His mouth dropped open in mock outrage. Grabbing my beer, he placed it on his desk along with his and then spun around to face me. "The betrayal!" He jabbed me in the chest. "I'm perfect, just the way I am."

I shrugged, a smile curving over my lips. "There's always room for improvement."

"You—" Without warning, he shoved my chest, sending me falling back onto his bed, and then he jumped on top of me. We wrestled like how I imagined two friends would wrestle, not that I had any experience, laughing and playfully shoving at each other.

"I can't...believe...you're fighting me...because I told you...the truth," I panted as he got me in a headlock. I threw my body back, trying to dislodge his grip, and everything came to a screaming halt.

There was something hard pressing against my ass, and I might've been inexperienced in all sex-related things, but I had a dick, and I instantly knew what I was feeling. I gasped at the same time Finn did, and we both scrambled away from each other. My face was on fire, and I didn't dare to look at Finn, but I had no doubt his was, too.

"Shit. Shitshitshit," he muttered to himself, all panicky breaths, making my heart rate go through the roof, and fuck, I needed to get out of there. It was the most awkward situation of both our lives.

"I...uh...essay. Forgot," I managed, not even waiting for a response before fleeing his house like the coward I was. Was it a huge overreaction? Yes, but what were you supposed to say to your friend when they got a boner from play wrestling with you? Was it a normal thing?

Back in my student flat in my bedroom with the door safely locked behind me, I forced myself to look at the situation more logically. Of the two of us, Finn was probably feeling the most weird about it. He'd been the one with a hard-on.

I did what I usually did when I was at a loss—typed the symptoms into Dr. Google.

Is it normal to get hard when you're wrestling?

My panic receded further as I scanned the results,

finding that yes, it was a normal reaction for some people due to the stimulation or friction or whatever. Now, I just needed to keep that in mind the next time I saw Finn. Fuck. It was going to be awkward either way. Maybe...

Switching on my computer, I loaded up *Lesath Legends* and then sent a text.

ME:

I'm online. Co-op battle for XP?

It took a couple of minutes, but then I received a thumbs up from Finn, and I jammed my headset over my mess of hair—speaking of, I seriously needed a haircut—and flipped on my mic.

"Hi." Finn's voice was low and more tentative than I'd ever heard it.

"Hi. Ready to go?"

"Yeah." He cleared his throat. "Uh, sorry about earlier. I-I don't—I didn't—"

The urge to reassure him came over me instantly. Was this how he felt when I was struggling to find the words? "It's a normal thing. It's the friction." That was, hands down, the most uncomfortable sentence I'd ever forced from my mouth, but it had to be said.

There was silence on the other end of the headset, and I busied myself with swapping out my character's weapons, hoping I hadn't made a mistake by directly addressing something that was clearly an incredibly awkward subject for us both.

Finally, though, Finn spoke. "Yeah. It's...normal. I'm sorry if...if I made you uncomfortable or anything, though."

"You didn't. It was just a surprise," I quickly said, wanting to reassure him, and he barked out a shocked laugh.

"A surprise. Right. Okay. Can we agree to never discuss it again?"

"*Please.*" I could count on one finger the number of people I could actually have a conversation like this with, and even with Finn, I never wanted to mention it again.

"Good. Uh, so, which co-op battle do you want to pick? The sand arena gives us an extra twenty percent XP if we make it through."

"You read my mind."

We settled into the game, falling into our usual synchronised rhythm, and I knew we were going to be okay.

EIGHT

FINN

L eo was nervous. I knew all the signs, and I'd expected them. But he was still here in the library. He'd come, and from the determined set of his jaw, he was going to see this through. I'd been mostly teasing when I called him "little lion," but it was true. Leo never failed to amaze me with how hard he tried. I wished he could see himself the way I saw him.

"They're gonna be here soon." His leg bounced next to mine, and I lowered my hand, placing it on his thigh. He stilled instantly.

"You've got this," I reassured him. "You've never backed out of a dare yet."

He shot me a smile that warmed me all over, grateful, like I'd said or done something amazing, when all I'd done was remind him he was capable of doing this. He gave me way too much credit and himself way too little.

I removed my hand from his thigh and busied myself with setting up my laptop. I was mostly here as emotional support, but there was the added bonus that Daisy was going to be there. Daisy, my teammate Pete's younger sister. Daisy, who was pretty and reciprocating my flirting efforts.

Daisy, who I hadn't thought about once since this whole thing had been arranged...

Sighing, I rubbed my hand over my face.

"Are you okay?"

The arrival of Charlie and the girls saved me from coming up with an answer to Leo's question. As they approached, Leo stiffened next to me, and I pressed my leg against his. He exhaled shakily and then raised his head.

"H-hi."

Charlie shot him an easy smile, then nodded at me. "Alright? Anyone want coffee? I'm going to the machine." He glanced at Sophie. "Soph? Wanna help me carry them?"

She smiled at him and nodded. After taking coffee orders, the two of them disappeared, and Daisy and Millie were left standing there, exchanging glances.

Right. The reason we were supposedly meeting in the library today was so Leo could help Millie set up a gallery for her photos, and here I was, taking up the only seat next to his.

I climbed to my feet, pulling out my chair. "Millie, why don't you sit here? Daisy, that means you get the pleasure of my company."

Daisy smiled at me as I pushed my stuff across the table and then took a seat opposite Leo. She drew me into a light-hearted conversation about football, and I relaxed as we debated the merits of the current Arsenal team versus Glevum FC in their upcoming match.

I kept finding my gaze sliding to Leo, though. Just to check if he was okay.

Charlie and Sophie returned, settling into the remaining chairs and handing out coffees to everyone. Daisy immediately began talking to Sophie, and I was free to check on my friend again.

Leo's brows were pulled together in concentration, his head bent close to Millie's as they both focused on her screen. "...So...you see here? Now we've got the empty gallery set up, all you need to do is drag and drop the photos and save here... Yeah, that's it. The website will automatically update."

"Finn? Finnegan!"

I blinked. "My name isn't Finnegan. Just Finn. It's not short for anything."

"Okay." Charlie's lips curved upwards in amusement. "Either way, I called your name five times before you noticed. Something interesting going on over there?" He gave a pointed glance towards Leo.

I shook my head insistently. "No. Just...thinking."

"Course you were. Anyway, all I wanted to say was, do you want to come..." He trailed off, his gaze flying to something behind me. I twisted in my seat to find Sophie's older brother, Nate, standing there, a coffee cup in one hand and the other clasping the strap of his bag.

And Charlie had the nerve to accuse *me* of being distracted.

Hang on. This was Sophie's brother, and Charlie and Sophie were interested in each other. I sat up in my seat, giving them my full attention, looking from Sophie to Charlie and then to Nate. Sophie was rolling her eyes at her brother, who was watching Charlie with an unreadable expression on his face. Charlie stared right back at him. He looked...flushed. I guess it was understandable. I'd never been subjected to the whole overprotective big brother routine and sadly hadn't been able to subject Ed to it, either, but I was sure it would be just as awkward as it looked right now.

"What are you doing here?" Sophie said after the silence stretched uncomfortably. I glanced back over at Leo, who hadn't even noticed the exchange, still engrossed with Millie's computer, and something inside me twisted. I tore my gaze away.

"It's the library. I'm using it for its intended purpose," Nate replied, still watching Charlie.

"Nate." Her tone was pleading, and it seemed to snap her brother out of it.

"Alright. I was just passing. I'll leave you to it." He stepped forwards, squeezing Sophie's shoulder. "See you later, okay?"

She relaxed, giving him a smile. "Yeah."

When he was gone, she sighed. "Older brothers. Right?"

"Right," Daisy agreed. "It's sweet that they want to look out for you, but they don't always seem to understand that we're adults now and we can be trusted to know our own minds."

"I'm an older brother, and my younger brother definitely can't be trusted to know his own mind," I joked. "Just kidding. He's alright."

"Leo? Do you have any siblings?"

My head jerked around, noticing Millie giving Leo a soft smile. She was leaning into him, her lashes lowered... yeah, she was definitely interested in my friend.

"Um. Y-yeah. I mean, no. I'm an only child." He gave her a tentative smile, and I found my mouth opening.

"Not true. You're an honorary Carsley at this point. My family has pretty much adopted you."

His gaze slid to mine, and his smile widened, reaching his eyes. I warmed all over. "That's true," he said.

"I'm an only child, too," Millie confided, drawing Leo's attention again. "Something else we have in common. Did you ever want siblings when you were growing up?"

"Charlie! What were you going to ask me earlier, before Sophie's brother showed up?" My voice came out way too loud, and judging by the amusement in Charlie's expression, he thought so, too.

"Oh, yeah! I was gonna say, do you want to come out on Saturday night? I was talking to JJ about Sanctuary because I've never been, and he said he'd get me and a few friends on the guest list if we wanted. What do you say? All of us?" His hand swept out, encompassing our table.

Daisy and Millie were instantly nodding, grinning at each other and Charlie. Leo's gaze caught mine.

I dare you, I mouthed, and he eyed me for a moment longer before he gave a tiny nod.

Lion, I mouthed again, and he bit back a smile.

"Okay," he said to Charlie.

"I'll be there." Obviously. Leo wouldn't go without me. Or would he? It seemed as if he was beginning to feel more comfortable around the others. Which was what I wanted. I didn't want him to need me as his security blanket or anything. Fuck knows he was more than capable. He just needed to see it for himself.

Sophie bit down on her lip. "I'd love to, but it's my cousin's birthday, and we're travelling to Swindon for the weekend. I'm definitely up for it another time, though. It sounds great."

"Yeah. We can sort something else out, don't worry," Charlie assured her, and based on the looks they were giving each other, I was pretty sure he meant that he'd sort out something a lot more private with her without the rest of us around.

Leo's bright laugh interrupted my thoughts, and it was so unexpected I stared at him, open-mouthed, before I got myself back under control. Millie was saying something to him, and the two of them looked so cosy...

It was good.

This was what I wanted.

Right?

"You did so good today. I'm really proud of you." I lay back on my bed, staring up at the ceiling.

The bed dipped, and Leo's face appeared in my field of vision, his brows pulled together as he stared down at me. "What's that voice for?"

"What voice?"

"Finn. Something's wrong, and I want to know what it is. Did I do something wrong? Did something happen when I was helping Millie with her website?"

Fuck. How could I explain to him what I couldn't even explain to myself?

Closing my eyes in the hope it would help me get the words out, I sighed. "It's not that. I am proud of you. I want you to know that. It's just that when Charlie invited everyone to the club and you said yes, it made me realise you didn't need me anymore."

"I—"

Fuck. My eyes flew open, and I reached up, covering his mouth. "Wait, no, let me finish. I know how fucked up that sounds. I don't want you to have to need me, but I guess...I guess I like being needed or something. But I don't want you to have to need me. Fuck. I just said that, didn't I?"

"Finn." His lips curved into a smile beneath my fingers. When I removed them, he raised his brows. "Hug?"

I nodded, stretching out my hand, and he collapsed onto his side next to me, slinging his arm across my stomach.

"I...I like being around you. I liked you being there today. It's not that I need you, or you're my security blanket, or I'm using you to make myself feel more confident. It's that I know I have you in my corner. Supporting me. It gives me the strength to push myself out of my comfort zone. Okay, maybe I do need you." He bit down on his lip, staring at me, before he moved closer, curling his body into mine.

His voice was muffled by the pillow when he spoke again. "I need you to be my friend and to push me. I need you to team up with me on our campaigns so we can get all the loot and XP. I need..."

He shot upright. "I need us to be a team. Or to keep being a team. Because we are a team, aren't we? Equals?"

I looked at him, and then I reached up, pulling him back down to me. "We're the best team. Hammerhead and his Viking. Who can stop us? No one on earth can possibly beat a shark *and* a Viking."

He laughed against my throat as I wrapped my arms around him, shifting so his torso was almost fully on top of me with his legs to the side, resting on the bed. I ran my hand down his back, and his fingers found their way into my hair, tugging lightly. I shivered.

His fingers immediately halted their movements. "Want me to stop?"

"No. It's nice." Sliding my hand into his hair, I twisted the strands between my fingers and pulled gently. "See?"

"Mmm." His head rose, his eyes meeting mine. "Is it weird for us to be doing this?"

I shrugged, jostling him. "Sorry. Uh, maybe it's weird, maybe it isn't, but I don't really care. Do you?"

"No. Just making sure." He laid his head back down again, his nose pressing into the side of my throat. "Finn?"

"Yeah?"

"I know I'm supposed to be interested in Millie, but I don't know if I am...I think...I don't really know how to be attracted to someone. What if I'm broken?"

My jaw tightened. "Don't ever think that. You're not broken. There's nothing wrong with you. Some people aren't attracted to anyone, ever. I can't remember the name, but it's a thing, and it's okay if it's you. I promise there's nothing wrong with you, Leo."

"Oh," he said quietly.

"Do you wanna skip the club?"

"No. I want to experience this. I want to go. With you. Just maybe...what if Millie wants to dance with me? Or more?"

"You're a great dancer. But you know you don't have to dance if you don't want to. You don't have to do anything you don't want to. You can say no."

"Yeah." He sighed. "I want to try, though. I just don't want to lead Millie on if I'm not interested. I mean, I guess I might be interested? I just... I'm not very good at recognising if I am or not. That probably makes no sense."

"It does make sense. Just remember, you don't have to do anything you don't want to. Ever."

A huff of breath hit the side of my throat. "Okay, if you say so."

"I do."

I tugged at his hair lightly, and he spoke up again. "I had

an idea. You know how I dared you to learn and perform a dance routine?"

"I was hoping you'd forgotten about that," I muttered, and he laughed.

"What if we do it for the club? It'll help me to focus on something, and it means you get to show off your new moves for Daisy."

For Daisy.

"Yeah, I guess so."

"Good. Let's make it official. I dare you, Finn Carsley, to learn a dance routine and perform it at Sanctuary on Saturday night."

With Leo's smile pressed against my neck and the happiness in his voice, how could I say anything but yes?

NINE

LEO

"Let me get this straight. You're going to teach the football player how to dance?" JJ's eyes sparkled with amusement.

I stared down at the studio floor, suddenly uncertain. Had this been a stupid idea?

"Hey. Leo. I didn't mean it like that. You're capable of doing it, you know that, right? It was just an image I had of Finn trying to dance." He waved his hand in the air. "It's not important."

"Do you really think I can do it?" Raising my head, I met his gaze. His eyes were warm, and he was smiling at me.

"Of course I do. Finn, I'm not so sure about. I only have his moves on the pitch to go by, so maybe he's got skills I don't know about. But if anyone can teach him, you can. You two have a special connection. He can get you to do things you wouldn't ordinarily do, so I'm sure it applies the other way around." He gave a decisive nod. "Yeah, if anyone can teach him, it's you."

"Thanks." I glanced up at the wall clock that hung

above the studio door. "I'm glad you think so because he'll be here in about five minutes."

"It's gonna be fine." JJ pulled me into a quick hug. "Promise."

"So this is what you get up to when I'm not around."

With a screech, I tore myself away from JJ to see Dr. Wilder standing in the doorway, two cups of coffee clasped in his hands. His mouth was curved into a smirk.

"Kill, stop scaring my friends, or I'll have to punish you," JJ announced, waltzing over to his boyfriend and swiping one of the cups from his grip. "Is this for me?"

"I'll be the one doing the punishing, my sunshine," he murmured, low and husky, and I saw JJ shiver. This was *so* awkward. I shuffled over to the far side of the studio, trying to act as if I was invisible, and exhaled with relief when JJ called out a goodbye and they left me alone.

"I found it! Your secret lair, where you hang out when you're not playing with computers."

My head shot up to see Finn grinning at me from the doorway, and I beckoned him inside.

"Excuse me, I do not play with computers. I do very important things with them."

"Course you do." He stepped into the studio and then stopped, seeming to take me in for the first time. He ducked his head, biting down on his lip, and my gaze shot to the mirror, examining myself. Did I have something on me?

Nope. Everything looked normal, as far as I could see. Messy red hair in serious need of a trim, black dance tights, loose sleeveless teal workout top...

Same old me.

I pointed towards my laptop, which was balancing on a small table in the corner of the studio. "This is a double dare today. I'm teaching you to dance, and you're teaching me confidence for the club. I spent a while researching the kind of dances people do at clubs because, um, I haven't exactly been to one before—" I grimaced. This was a stupid idea, wasn't it?

"You researched club dancing?" Stepping up behind me, so close I could feel his body heat, Finn smiled at my reflection in the mirror. "So sweet."

"Hey!"

"I wasn't taking the piss. The fact you took the time to do that. It's sweet." He squeezed my bicep, pressing his chest against my back for a second before stepping away. "Okay. Let me know what I need to do." I watched in the mirror as he tugged his hoodie off, his T-shirt riding up as he did so. I caught a glimpse of defined abs before he yanked it back down. My heart rate was increasing for some reason, and we hadn't even started dancing yet.

I cleared my throat, glancing back at my laptop. "It's better if we go barefoot, I think. Shoes off, then come over here." This was already weird. I'd been dancing for a while, but I'd never tried to teach anyone else what to do. Teaching involved a whole different skill set, and I just hoped I could get through this session without making a fool of myself. At least this was Finn. He'd understand if I messed up.

Finn came up next to me, and I hit Play on the video I'd bookmarked. It was a compilation of clips of dancers doing different routines to the same song. When we reached the clip I wanted to focus on, I paused the video.

"Watch this one. I thought we could learn this dance. The steps are fairly simple, so I don't think you'll have any trouble picking them up, and based on the research I did, it should work as a club dance, too." Hitting Play again, we watched the clip, and then I went through it again at a slower speed, pointing out the footwork and arm placements. Finn sighed next to me, reaching up to rub at his face.

"This seems complicated. How do you remember all the steps, and how to hold yourself, and all that?"

"Lots of practice. Don't worry, I'm not expecting you to get it straight away." His expression was still hesitant, so I added, "I'm not expecting it to be perfect, either. And, Finn? This is meant to be fun, but if you're not into it or don't want to do it, I'm not going to force you."

He turned to me then. "I do want to do this. It's just all a bit overwhelming."

"I have faith in you," I told him. It was weird for me to be the one reassuring him he could do something, but it was nice, and when he gave me a small smile, it made something inside me warm.

We went through a series of warm-ups, and then I got the music ready.

"Watch me go through it once, then I'll break it down for you." I could already feel my face heating because Finn was so close, watching me so intently. No one else had ever been this close and watched me like this other than JJ and Alyssa, who were dancers themselves, so it didn't count.

Finn nodded, leaning back against the mirror with his hands shoved into the pockets of his black joggers. Swallowing my nerves, I started up the music track and then began to move. The steps were simple, and the entire short routine I'd planned to teach him was only around twelve seconds long—which, okay, to a non-dancer still might be a little daunting, but I was going to do my best to break it all down for him in the easiest possible way.

When I was done, I stopped the music and looked over at Finn.

"So?" I said eventually, after he just stared at me. It was a little unnerving.

"Did— You're amazing," he said, his voice a little hoarse. Clearing his throat, he lowered his gaze, scuffing his toe on the floor. "Yeah. Amazing."

"Stop embarrassing me." I covered my face with my hands, and I heard his soft chuckle. A warm huff of breath skated over my skin, and then his fingers were curling around mine, prying them away from my face.

"You're ridiculous," he said, wrapping his arms around me. My arms automatically went around his back, and I hooked my chin over his shoulder.

"You're the ridiculous one. You've seen me dance before," I mumbled, pressing my nose into the side of his face. Whatever his shampoo was, it smelled good. Like apples and a hint of spice. Apple pie, maybe.

I heard, or felt, his breath hitch. "A-are you sniffing me?" His voice had a bit of a crack to it.

"Sorry. Your shampoo? Whatever it is. It smells nice."

He let out a shaky laugh, releasing me, and I might have been imagining it, but the atmosphere in the room had changed, grown heavier in a way I couldn't even begin to describe.

Fucking hell, Leo. Why did you have to make it weird? Friends don't sniff each other's hair.

"Sorry," I said again. "Clearly, I need more practice in how to be normal."

"Leo. Don't speak about yourself like that." Gripping my chin, he nudged it upwards, so I had no choice but to look at him. His brows pulled together, and then he suddenly darted forwards, pressing a kiss to the side of my head.

A kiss?

When he moved back, my face wasn't the only one that was flushed.

"There. We're even now," he said.

"Did—did you just kiss my hair?"

"Uh, yeah." He shifted on his feet, shoving his hands back into his pockets. "It tops you sniffing my hair in the weirdness department, right?"

I thought about it for a minute, a smile spreading across my face as I realised he'd done it to make me feel less awkward. My entire body relaxed, and I felt like I could breathe properly again.

"I dunno. Sniffing your friend's hair is definitely weirder than kissing them. Friends kiss platonically."

"You're the only friend I've kissed," he told me, his face going even redder, and I just wanted to comfort him, to make him feel better. Was this how he felt with me?

"That's because I'm your best friend. Special privileges." Fuck. Did he consider me his best friend? I definitely considered him as mine.

His gaze shot to mine, and a tiny, reluctant smile tugged at his lips. "Yeah. You are my best friend," he said seriously.

"I've never had a best friend before."

"*Leo.*" He lunged forwards, hugging me again, but it was over as quickly as it had started. He cleared his throat again. "Okay. Enough of that. Let's get on with this dance. I've got a lecture in fifty minutes, and it's probably gonna take you that long to teach me the first move."

"Yeah." Straightening up, I restarted the music. "Let's do this."

TEN

FINN

Sanctuary was unlike any club I'd ever been in. Everything about it was high-end, from the rich midnight blues and deep blacks to the burnished gold accents. As I pushed through the crowds towards the bar, my fingers wrapped around Leo's wrist so we didn't lose each other, I reminded myself of why I was here. For Leo. And to a lesser extent, for my dare, to perform my dance in front of people.

And the girls. Speaking of...

There they were, drinks in hand, standing around a high table with Charlie and my teammates Freddie and Levi, as well as Levi's boyfriend, Asher. Charlie noticed me first, and I lifted my hand in acknowledgement before pointing to the bar and miming myself drinking. He gave me a thumbs up, and I continued to weave through the crowds, tugging Leo with me until we reached the bar.

Releasing Leo's wrist, I placed my hand on his back, leaning in to be heard over the thumping music.

"What do you want to drink?"

He stared around us, wide-eyed, before shaking his

head. "I have no clue. This is my first time in a club. I-I don't—"

Fuck, his whole body had completely stiffened, and was that panic in his eyes? I slid my hand from his back to the side of his waist so my arm was curled around him, and he immediately leaned into me.

"I'll choose," I assured him, and he nodded, some of the tension leaving him. Keeping it simple, I ordered us two beers, which were ridiculously expensive compared to the prices in my usual student haunts, and I was glad I hadn't gone with anything more complex.

Turning his head so his lips brushed over my ear, he murmured a soft "Thanks," accepting the drink, and I suppressed a weird shiver.

Get a fucking grip, Finn. Drawing back from him, I gripped his wrist again, leading him over to the table where the others were waiting for us.

"You made it!" Daisy threw her arms around me, and after a second where I stood there frozen, completely unprepared for her level of friendliness, I patted her back with my free hand. Over her shoulder, I saw Millie *blatantly* eye-fucking Leo, who was giving her a shy smile.

I gritted my teeth.

Okay, my friend looked good tonight. I'd helped him pick out the outfit. He'd kept it simple, with dark jeans and a plain black sleeveless T-shirt. He'd wrapped a leather band studded with silver around his wrist, and he'd done something with his hair to make it look, in his words, "less of an overgrown mess." I liked his hair as it was anyway, but whatever product he'd used was making the red and gold tones seem like they were almost glowing. With his huge green eyes, all that pale skin, those freckles scattered across the bridge of his nose and cheeks, his defined cheekbones and plush lips... He was fucking hot. I could admit that. Not that I'd say it aloud because that would be a whole other awkward mess, and I didn't want anyone getting the wrong idea.

Anyway, the point was, yes, he looked good, but did Millie have to eye-fuck him that obviously? Didn't she know she was making him feel uncomfortable?

Or was she? Absentmindedly releasing Daisy, I studied them. No, Leo was actually leaning into Millie, his smile widening as she said something in his ear.

My jaw tightened. Spinning away, I greeted the boys, diving into a conversation about our upcoming match against Greenwich Uni. Daisy happily joined in, and she had several surprisingly good insights for someone who didn't play. It turned out that as well as having a football-playing brother, she and Sophie had both played on a girls' football team when they were younger. They'd gone to the same school, along with Millie, who hadn't played football but who had religiously attended every one of their games to support them.

So, to recap. Daisy. Very pretty. Knew a lot about the sport I played. A nice, supportive friend. Athletic—which was my type, according to Ander. All the boxes were being ticked, and I couldn't work out why I wasn't more intrigued by her.

I was a lost fucking cause tonight, too in my head, worrying about Leo. Daisy deserved better, and with that in mind, I decided to be a good wingman. I'd seen the way Charlie's friend Freddie had been looking at her—the same way Millie was looking at Leo—and so I turned to him.

"Hey, Freddie. Have you told Daisy about the initiation thing you did for her brother Pete when he joined the first team?"

They smiled at each other, and I stepped back.

"Bar," I said, holding up my beer bottle, which was still mostly full. Without waiting for anyone to answer me, I pushed into the crowds, losing myself in a sea of anonymous bodies while I tried to get my head together. I drank as I walked, making a circuit around the large dance floor. Reaching a roped-off set of glass stairs leading upwards, I paused. Charlie had mentioned something about a VIP area, so I guessed I'd found the entrance. The bouncer standing at the bottom of the stairs shot me a look that clearly communicated "don't even think about it," so I continued my circuit, coming back up to the table. Leo was still deep in conversation with Millie, and I was honestly so fucking relieved and proud of him. I knew he'd be okay, but something inside me settled, seeing the visual proof in front of me.

Millie noticed me approach, and she said something to Leo, who looked up. When our eyes met, he smiled, wide and bright and happy, and I got weirdly emotional. This was how he should always be. Happy.

"Anyone wanna dance?" Charlie suggested when I reached the others. I glanced over at Leo, who was nodding, and so I ditched my beer bottle and followed everyone onto the dance floor. We found a relatively empty space and shuffled around to the music until Levi muttered something and disappeared. He came back with a tray of shots, the tiny glasses brimming with something green and lethal-looking, and instructed us all to drink them. He'd got us two each, and they burned as they went down. My eyes watered after the first one, and after the second, I was coughing, but I could feel the alcohol taking effect almost straight away.

Ten minutes later, we were all properly dancing, and there was no doubt about it—Leo was the centre of attention. The way he moved was so fucking graceful, despite our recent shots, and he didn't even seem to notice that everyone was watching him. He was lost in the music, in his own world, and it made me so happy.

That was, until he came back to himself, and his eyes widened. His gaze snapped to mine, and he crooked his finger at me. Charlie was saying something, but I wasn't paying attention, moving towards Leo and watching his smile grow bigger as I drew closer. When I reached him, he threw his arms around me, and I automatically hugged him back, my alcohol-infused brain not caring how it looked to anyone else.

"You have to dance. You promised," he slurred into my ear, and, oh. Yeah.

"Do I have to?"

"It was a *dare*."

"Okay, okay." Releasing him, I shook my head. "I can't believe you're making me do this right now."

His smile disappeared. "You don't have to do anything you don't want to," he said immediately. Okay, he slurred it, but I understood exactly what he meant.

"It's okay. I never back out of a dare." What was the worst that could happen? Everyone was tipsy, and I'd either amuse them or, more likely, baffle them.

Moving into the centre of our loose circle, I held up my hand. "Alright. Who wants to see my moves?"

"What moves?" Charlie called, and I laughed. Counting under my breath, I began, going through the steps just like Leo had taught me.

Twelve seconds felt like hours, but I made it through, and when I was done, I gave a theatrical bow to the sound of my friends applauding me. Leo was grinning as he clapped, his eyes sparkling, and I returned his grin, giving him a thumbs up.

"Good job," Charlie said, passing out another round of shots. "I didn't know you had it in you."

"I didn't, but Leo helped me out," I admitted.

"You two are close, aren't you?" he said, and something in his voice had my eyes narrowing.

"What's that supposed to mean?"

"Nothing at all."

An arm flung itself over my shoulders, and the next second, I had a drunken Leo pressed up against me.

"You did it! You were sooo good."

Charlie smirked at me, and mouthed, *See. Close.* I gave him the finger. Leo's and my friendship was no one's business but our own.

"I won't be giving you a run for your money anytime soon, but I did alright," I said to Leo, wrapping my arm around his waist for balance. His, and mine. When I thought about it, it was a miracle that I'd executed all the steps correctly.

He leaned into me, his mouth touching my ear. "Can I come home with you tonight? Connor's not around this weekend."

"Course you can."

"Can we go soon? I don't feel very good."

Shit. Drawing back, I eyed him cautiously. His eyes were glassy, and yeah...he looked a bit green.

"That last shot was a bit much, huh?"

He nodded slowly, his mouth twisting into a grimace. "It just hit me. I feel sick."

"Okay. Let's get you home."

After assurances from the others that they'd stick together and make sure everyone got home okay, I ordered an Uber to my house. Leo spent the entire time curled into a ball, groaning and saying he felt sick, but we made it back without him actually throwing up. When we got inside the house, I downed a pint of water and made myself a strong coffee in the hope I could sober up enough myself to take care of him. I was feeling more or less normal by the time I got him up to my room with a glass of water and a bucket.

While I'd been getting the bucket, he'd managed to kick off his jeans and collapse in a starfish position on my bed in his T-shirt and underwear, groaning into my pillow.

"Sorry," he mumbled when I sat down next to him, brushing his hair back from his face. "I ruined your night."

"You ruined nothing. Drink this water." I helped him to sit up, and he obediently drank from the glass before collapsing back down again with another groan.

"I made you leave."

"You didn't make me do anything, and I don't care that we left early. We had a good time, didn't we? We did everything we wanted to do. You got me to show off my new dance moves."

"Yeah." He buried his face in my pillow again. "Can you lie with me? The room's spinning, and I need to hold on to something."

"Okay. Let me get the light." I tugged off my jeans and T-shirt and turned off the lamp. I opened the curtains just enough to allow a bit of light from the streetlamps to filter in, so Leo could see what he was doing if he needed to get up or was sick or anything. Grabbing a clean T-shirt, I pulled it over my head and then carefully climbed onto the bed, trying not to jostle Leo. When I was settled next to him on my back, he shifted positions, curling into my side.

"Thank you."

I curled my arm around him. "Anytime. You'd do the same for me."

"I would." He yawned, unsuccessfully attempting to burrow his head into my shoulder muscle. "Finn?"

"Yeah?"

"I think Millie might want to kiss me. Would...would you be able to teach me how?"

Everything stuttered to a halt. I couldn't think. Couldn't breathe.

"Finn? I dare you."

Fuck.

"Ask me again when you're sober," I said eventually, but he was already asleep.

I lay awake for a long time.

ELEVEN

LEO

I buried my face in my arms. "I'm never drinking again."

Finn's dad chuckled. "We've all been there. Eat this, it'll help."

Raising my head, I cautiously eyed the plate in front of me. Bacon, eggs, and HP sauce sandwiched between two thick slices of white bread. Okay. One bite. I could do this.

One bite turned into two and then three, and by the time I'd cleared my plate, I was feeling much better. That came with a side effect, though. Now I could think properly, the memories of last night were rushing back.

I couldn't believe I'd propositioned Finn in my drunken state. Daring him to dance was one thing, but daring him to kiss me? That was a line I shouldn't have crossed, and now I'd made things awkward. We'd barely even spoken this morning. Finn was already out of bed by the time I'd woken. He'd appeared to sort me out with a towel and change of clothes so I could shower and directed me to come downstairs for breakfast when I was ready, but that had been the extent of our interactions. It felt like there was a new distance between us, and it was one I'd put there with my thoughtless, drunken words.

That meant we needed to talk, and I was already dreading it.

"Another cuppa?" Finn's dad asked.

"No, thank you. But thanks. For all of this," I said, trying to swallow around the lump in my throat. This whole family had become important to me, and I didn't want to lose them.

He studied me, frowning, and then he reached forwards, placing his hand on my shoulder.

"Leo, I hope you know that we all consider you to be part of our family. I'm just doing what I'd do for my other sons, and you don't need to thank me for it."

"I-I know. Thank you," I said again, trying to convey everything I meant with my words. I wasn't sure how I'd managed to get so lucky.

A smile spread across his face. "Alright. You're welcome. Now, you can do me a favour. Go and have a word with Finn, would you? He seems a bit out of sorts this morning, and I'm sure you're just the person to cheer him up."

"Um." I licked my lips. "Yeah. I'll try."

"Good lad." He squeezed my shoulder and then stepped away, and I took that as my cue to leave.

Should I play it off as a drunken mistake, as words that I didn't really mean? The thing was, I *did* want Finn to teach me how to kiss. There was no one else I trusted. I'd meant what I said last night, that I thought Millie might want to kiss me, and although I wasn't sure if I wanted to kiss her, I wanted to be prepared in case things changed.

I'd never walked up a set of stairs more slowly in my life. Trying to drag it out, I detoured to the bathroom and gave my teeth the kind of deep clean I only bothered with before a visit to the dentist, but eventually, it got to a point where I couldn't put it off any longer. Standing outside Finn's room, my heart pounding, I took several deep breaths, doing my best to push back my rising anxiety.

"You don't have to hang around outside the door." Finn's voice was resigned but amused. "Come here."

I steeled myself and walked into his room, closing the door behind me. The distance between his door and his gaming chair had never seemed so short. Why was time speeding up when I needed it to slow down?

I stared down at his socked feet and navy joggers, and I swallowed. This was Finn. My best friend. The person who didn't judge me.

"ImeantwhatIsaidlastnight," I rushed out before I could lose my nerve.

"Leo."

Encouraged by the soft, fond way he said my name, I tried again. "I-I meant it. Only if you're okay with it."

"You really want me to teach you how to kiss?"

I risked a glance at him. He was staring down at his knees, his brow furrowed.

"Not if you're uncomfortable with it."

His head lifted, and his eyes met mine. I couldn't read his expression, but his words were firm. Commanding.

"Dare me."

Oh, fuck. This had been so much easier when my anxiety had been dulled by those shots.

"I. Um. I dare you to teach me how to kiss."

He didn't respond with words.

His hands came out, settling at my sides, and then he tugged me forwards to straddle him. Suddenly, I was sitting on his thighs, with his deep blue eyes intent on mine, our faces so close that I could see his individual lashes, the way his pupils dilated as he moved even closer...

One of his hands left my side, coming up to cup my jaw, and then he spoke, his words a low rasp. "Don't think. Just feel. Follow my lead."

Slowly, he leaned forwards, brushing his lips against mine so gently. I did my best to copy his movements, our lips moving together awkwardly. Until I somehow got the hang of it and managed to match his rhythm, and then it wasn't awkward anymore. It was all closed-mouth, and I knew that open-mouthed was the most likely scenario if I were to kiss anyone else, but I didn't know how that could possibly be an improvement on this.

"Okay?" he murmured, and I hummed in acknowledgement, kissing him again. He let me explore his mouth, and as my confidence grew, so did his. He did a thing with his teeth on my lower lip that felt so good, and I immediately wanted to try it on him. I carefully tugged his bottom lip between my teeth, feeling the way it was both soft and firm, and then I brought my hands up to wrap around his nape as I pressed tentative kisses to the corners of his lips.

When I drew back, we were both breathing heavily. My entire body was tingling. It was like nothing I'd ever felt before.

I felt his hands trembling where he was holding me. "Finn? Are you okay? Are you sure you don't mind doing this?"

He immediately shook his head. "It's not that. I just...I want to make it good for you."

"It's not like I'd know the difference, but it is good."

"Yeah, but it's your first kiss, even if it's only practice. I want it to be good for you."

I pressed my forehead against his. "It's good, Finn. Promise."

"Okay. Okay." Drawing back, his eyes met mine, his pupils wide and dark. "Wanna try it with tongues?" he suggested. His voice was so fucking husky it made me shiver. I'd never heard him sound quite like that before. It was new and different, and I...I liked it.

"Uh...sure." I licked my lips. "How do we do this?"

"Just follow my lead. We'll take it slow."

My whole body was trembling as he leaned in again. Our lips met, and he slowly coaxed my mouth open with a careful brush of his tongue along the seam of my lips. Doing my best to follow his movements, I gasped as our tongues slid together, the sensation like nothing I'd ever felt before.

Finn tried to pull back at my gasp, but I tightened my grip on him, holding him in place, and I felt his lips curve into a smile. Then we were kissing again, experimenting with presses of tongue, everything soft and slow and so, so good. I was breathless, dizzy, the tingles in my body spreading everywhere, a fluttering feeling in my stomach as Finn held me so carefully, kissing me and kissing me and kissing me.

Eventually, though, he gently pulled away. With a shaky exhale, he tipped his head back and rubbed his hand over his face, his eyes still closed.

"Fucking hell," he mumbled.

A tendril of anxiety curled through the euphoria I was feeling. Was that a good "fucking hell" or a bad one? Before I could spiral, he stroked his hand down my back.

"I can feel you thinking. Don't start worrying. You were...fuck. You're a natural."

I smiled. "I did okay? Really?"

"Millie, or whoever you kiss for real, is gonna be one lucky person," he said, and his voice sounded strange.

"Thanks." I didn't want to think about kissing anyone else. Not yet.

With a sigh, he released me, directing me to stand. "Be back in a second," he muttered, swinging himself off the chair and turning his back to me almost straight away. As he left the room, I flopped back on his bed, my head still spinning. It took a while for my breathing to go back to normal.

If that was what kissing was like, I'd been missing out.

More practice was definitely needed.

To improve my skills.

Practice makes perfect, after all.

TWELVE

FINN

S o. Apparently, kissing was a thing we did now. For practice. According to today, anyway, three days after the first practice kiss. We'd had two hours of gaming after spending an hour working on our respective assignments. After we'd completed a campaign we'd been attempting to finish for a while, Leo had suggested that we should celebrate with a movie. We'd curled up on my bed with a bowl of popcorn, and about five minutes into the film, Leo had looked over at me.

"Finn?"

"Yeah?"

He bit down on his lip, his cheeks flushing. "Never mind."

"Little lion." The nickname slipped so easily from my mouth, despite it originally being more of a tease than a proper nickname. "Tell me."

"I was thinking...I need more practice kissing. I've only done it once, and if you don't mind—"

"I don't mind." Twisting my body, I reached for him, curving my hand around his nape. There was no need for him to reply. We were both on the same page, our lips meeting, and it was just as good as the first time we'd done this.

It was too good.

It was fucking killing me.

We were now an hour into the movie, and we'd kissed another two times after the first one. We'd ended up reclined on the bed, my torso propped up with three pillows while Leo curled into my side, his fingertips tracing over my knuckles. I'd thrown a blanket over our lower halves, and I'd pulled one of my legs up a bit, purely because these kisses were having a very unwelcome side effect on my dick.

What would Leo think of me if he knew I was getting hard from his kisses? And it wasn't only his kisses that were having this effect on me, if I was honest with myself. If I had any sense, I'd pull away, draw a line that we shouldn't cross, cut out the cuddling and kissing. But I knew it would upset him, and I was too selfish to stop. I wanted to keep kissing him. I wanted to wrap him in my arms. I wanted to lie on my bed, bantering with my best friend and to know he was comfortable enough around me to share things he wouldn't share with anyone else.

I couldn't. Fucking. Stop.

Each time Leo gave me *the look*, his green eyes wide and hopeful, his lips slightly parted like he was already preparing for us to kiss, I couldn't help leaning in. It was like a compulsion. And the weirdest part about it was that it wasn't weird at all. Just like everything else in our relationship, it felt so natural. Normal.

I ran my fingers through his soft, tousled hair, enjoying the warmth and closeness of his presence. He breathed out, tapping my knuckle with his index finger.

"Finn. Thank you for doing all this. Really. It means a lot."

"You know I'll do anything for you," I said instantly. *I'm doing it for me, too,* was my unspoken admission. My mouth kept going, words I hadn't planned to say spilling out unchecked. "Want to practise kissing some more?"

He nodded against me, shifting around and raising himself onto one elbow. His hand went to my cheek, and he rubbed his thumb across my stubble.

"Guess I won't be dealing with this if I end up kissing any girls."

Nausea churned inside me, and I had to swallow several times before I could respond to him.

"I need a shave," was all I managed to say, but it made him smile.

"It suits you. Shaved or stubble. You look good either way."

I felt my cheeks heating at his simply stated comment. Fucking hell, it was like I'd never been complimented before. My brain wasn't working enough to give me words for a reply, so instead, I lifted my head and kissed him again.

"Ugh! Bro, that's grim! My eyes!"

We sprang apart so fast that I almost fell off the bed, throwing out my arms at the last second to stabilise myself.

My brother stood in my doorway, smirking as he pretended to scrub at his eyes.

"Haven't you ever heard of knocking?" I'd thought my face was hot before, but it was at volcano levels now.

"I did knock, but I guess you two were too busy." Ed puckered his lips, making the most obnoxious kissing sounds. "I was gonna see if either of you could help me decide on the photo I should submit for my assignment, but—"

"We'll help," Leo said immediately, pulling himself upright. I glanced over at him, noting how flushed he was, but other than that, he didn't seem too concerned that Ed had just caught us kissing. Now I thought about it, Ed didn't seem that bothered, either. Weird. Leo, I could understand because he could've assumed that I'd spoken to my brother about the kissing practice—which I hadn't—but Ed? I needed to have a word with him in private.

Needed to...but I knew I'd be putting that awkward conversation off for as long as possible.

"Cool, thanks." He crossed the room to my bed, throwing himself down between us. It was only then that I noticed he had his laptop clasped under his arm. Opening the lid, he tapped on the screen. "Okay. I narrowed it down to four, and they're all gonna be in my final portfolio, but I need to pick the standout photo to blow up big and mount."

Leo shifted forwards, his brows pulling together as he focused on the screen while Ed went through each of the images. It was so fucking cute that he was so invested in my brother's schoolwork, and—

Cute. Really, Finn?

"Fuck's sake," I mumbled to myself. They both turned to look at me in unison, and I quickly shook my head. "Not that. Don't worry. Uh, I like the waterfall photo best."

Ed frowned. "You don't think it's a bit cliché?"

"I like the shoe one," Leo said. "It's like you're an ant or something, and you're about to get stepped on. The black and white makes it more dramatic, too."

A huge grin spread across my brother's face, and he fist pumped the air. "Yeah! That's exactly what I was going for! I did the underside of the boot, so it looks like you're about to be splatted beneath it." He clapped his hands together, making a splatting sound for effect. "Yeah. That's the one. Thanks, Leo."

Closing the lid of his laptop with a slam that made me

wince, he hopped off the bed. With a salute and another bright smile, he disappeared, closing the door behind him.

"I'm—"

The door flew open again, and Ed strode back into the room, swiped the bowl of popcorn from where I'd left it on my bedside table, and then walked out again. He paused in the doorway. "Gonna need sustenance for the all-nighter I'm about to pull. This saves me going down to the kitchen. Thanks, bro. Bros."

After he'd gone, I waited a minute before I spoke again, just to make sure he wasn't going to come bursting back into the room. When my door remained closed, I collapsed back on my bed with a groan.

"Sorry."

Leo smiled. "I don't mind helping him. We weren't really watching the movie, anyway, were we?"

We both glanced towards my TV. Honestly, after I'd started kissing Leo, I'd kind of forgotten we were watching anything.

"Yeah. Not about that. Sorry that...uh, that he saw us kissing."

Leo bit down on his lip. "He didn't seem that surprised, so I assumed you'd told him about us practising."

"No. I definitely did not tell my nosy brother about that. I wouldn't, not without checking if you were okay with him knowing first. I wouldn't even think of telling him at all, to be honest."

"Oh. Well, I guess he found out somehow. I guess...I don't mind him knowing about that. I know the two of you like to rile each other up, but you don't mean it, do you? I trust him. He's a good guy."

"Yeah, he is," I said softly. "He knows when to back off, and believe it or not, he can actually be discreet when it matters. He'd never knowingly do anything to upset you, either."

"Okay, then it's not a problem."

I shook my head. How was Leo taking this so well? Fuck, he'd changed so much in the time I'd known him. Around my family, especially. It really did feel like he was part of the family.

"If you're sure."

"I'm sure." Leo patted the bed. "Can we pretend to watch the rest of the movie?"

I took the hint, moving back into my original reclined position, and Leo smiled, curling back into my body again as if it were the most natural thing in the world.

It wasn't long before his breathing slowed and his body went lax against me. It took me a while longer to fall asleep with so many thoughts running through my mind, but eventually, I succumbed, too.

THIRTEEN

FINN

"Leo?"

"Hmmm?" He was staring at the TV screen, not really paying me any attention, but I'd just received a text from Travis, the LSU football captain...

"I dare you to come to a team night with me."

Leo's eyes widened, and he turned to face me. "Why? I-I'm not part of the team, or—"

"I dare you to come with me."

He looked torn. "How many people will be there? What happens at a team night? Where is it?"

I tapped out a reply to Travis, asking who else was going. When my phone buzzed again, I scanned the text.

"Travis doesn't know exact numbers because he said it depends on who brings friends or partners, but it won't be the whole team. He says it's gonna be a quiet one at his house, just gaming and chilling. I thought it could be a good thing. There'll be enough people there that you won't feel obligated to make conversation, and it'll be relaxed, not like a party or anything. What do you think? Are you gonna accept my dare?"

"C-can we leave if it gets too much?"

Pulling him into me, I kissed the side of his head. It was getting far too easy to act like this around him. Half the time, I did it without even thinking—it was like a natural action that just happened. "We can leave whenever you want. You don't even have to give a reason. Just say the word, and we'll go."

His arms came around my waist. He sighed. "Okay. I'll come."

So much for it being a quiet one. It seemed like most of the team had shown up at Travis' house, and nearly everyone had brought someone with them. All the sofas and chairs were occupied, so I lowered myself to the floor in front of the TV, stretching out my legs in front of me. I nodded to Bennett, sprawled out next to me with Niccolò curled up in his lap.

"Alright, Ben?"

"Yeah. Tired. Did you finish the sustainability coursework?"

I shook my head. "Not yet. I think I'm about halfway through. You?"

"I'm almost done with mine, but I could do with another set of eyes on it. Want to read through each other's work when we're finished?"

"Yeah, that sounds good." I meant to continue speaking, but my attention was diverted by Travis calling my best friend's name.

"Leo! You're up next!"

My head swung to where Leo was leaning against the wall with JJ, who had apparently been dragged here by

Niccolò. They'd been talking in a quiet corner ever since we'd arrived, and I'd been happy to leave Leo to it, knowing he'd message or come and find me if he needed me.

"M-me?" Leo stammered, his cheeks flushing, and I had to fight back the physical urge to go to him and wrap him up and hide him away from the world.

"Yeah, you're up. It's you, Niccolò, Liam, and Preston. Winner goes into the next round." Travis tapped the whiteboard he'd been using to plot out the *Mario Kart* rounds. We'd been randomly divided into groups of four and were taking turns to play a round. The overall winner would go into the second round, and so on, until everyone was eliminated. There was a crate of beer up for grabs for the winner, although for a group of footballers, it was the thrill of the competition we liked. And the winning, naturally.

Leo's gaze flew to mine, and I nodded encouragingly. I saw him square his shoulders, and then he moved, crossing the room towards me with his gaze fixed on mine. As he drew near, I saw his eyes darting around, a panicked expression coming over his face, and I instantly realised what had him so stressed.

Widening my legs, I patted the newly created space in between them. It meant that my thighs were pressed against Bennett on one side and against a chair leg on the other, but the minimal discomfort was worth it to see the relieved expression on Leo's face as he stepped over several pairs of legs and lowered himself down in front of me.

My arms came around him straight away, and his body melted into mine as he exhaled a shaky breath.

"Okay?" I murmured in his ear, and he nodded against me, accepting the controller Travis handed to him. When I glanced up at Travis, he was staring between us with his brows raised. Okay, I knew how this probably looked to him, but it wasn't like that.

Fuck off, I mouthed discreetly, and he smirked at me before turning his attention to Niccolò, who stared at his controller blankly before asking Bennett how he was supposed to use it. With the attention away from me and Leo, I relaxed a little, pulling Leo closer and tucking my chin over his shoulder so I could see the action on the screen more easily.

"Okay. Rules. I know we went through them before, but I'll repeat them each time so everyone's clear about what we're doing," Travis said.

"Thanks, Dad!" came Liam's shout from the sofa behind me, and Travis gave him the finger before continuing.

"50cc race, Mario Kart Stadium. Your choice of vehicle and driver. Next round will be 100cc, so I don't want to hear any more complaints about these rounds being too slow, *Ander.*"

"I'm built for speed!" Ander called, and Liam laughed.

"I feel sorry for your boyfriend. If you want any tips about slowing down and making it good for him, I'm happy to advise."

"Fuck you, Holmes. I feel sorry for Noah, having to be dicked down by a sloth."

They both dissolved into laughter while Travis rolled his eyes.

"Is this what it's always like?" Leo whispered to me, and I could hear the amusement in his voice.

"Sometimes, yeah." Most of the time, probably.

I reached up, brushing aside some of Leo's hair that was tickling my cheek, and he stiffened.

"I need a haircut."

"I like your hair. It was just tickling my face. It looks good, though. I love the colour."

He twisted around to stare at me, his eyes wide. "You do?"

"Yeah, I do."

"Me too," came a voice from next to us, and we turned in unison to see Niccolò, the little eavesdropper, smiling brightly at us. "It's so pretty. I tried to dye mine that colour, but it didn't turn out like I wanted it." He pouted, and Bennett was quick to kiss his cheek, instantly wiping his pout away.

"Oh. Um. Thanks." Leo gave the floor a shy smile and then twisted back around, settling into his original position against my chest. He seriously was so fucking cute.

Brain. Stop.

Thankfully for my brain, the game started up. Leo leaned forwards, intent on the screen as the countdown started. Next to us, Nic had persuaded Bennett to take his turn, Bennett's arms coming around him to hold the controller, while Nic gave "helpful" advice about mushrooms and shells, but Leo didn't pay them any attention. It reminded me of when we were gaming together, how wrapped up he could get in a campaign, and it was like the outside world no longer existed.

Leo won the race easily, grinning against me as he sailed across the finish line, almost half a lap ahead of the others.

"What the fuck! How did you manage to get that far ahead?" Liam shouted from behind us, and I laughed. Because Leo was now burrowing into me, doing his best to become invisible, I replied for him, twisting so I could see Liam while I held Leo in place with my arm.

"Sore loser, Liam?"

He smirked at me. "Think you can do better? You're up

next. And you're up against my boyfriend, who's the unde-feated champion."

I shrugged. "Can't make any promises, but I'll give it my best shot."

When I turned around again, Leo leaned into me, his head tilting to the side so he could speak into my ear. "Do you want me to move?"

No.

"Nah, you're good there, if you're comfortable."

"Okay."

Alright, it was a little harder to play when I had to stretch my arms around Leo, and yeah, I didn't win—the honour went to Noah—but I came a respectable second. Now I was out, I could relax and enjoy Leo. I mean, enjoy my friends, which obviously included Leo.

Leo, who made it through to the final round. It was him against Noah, Travis, and Kira, Travis' girlfriend, and obvi-ously, I was rooting for my lion. JJ was, too, which meant Niccolò was, and that meant Bennett was cheering him on, too. My face ached from smiling so much, seeing the way people were cheering for my friend, and how he seemed quietly pleased, flushed and biting back small smiles as he kept his gaze fixed on the screen. Tonight had gone so much better than I could have imagined, and I was so happy.

"You've got this," I whispered in Leo's ear before giving in to my instincts and pressing a quick kiss to his hair. I mean, my mouth was right there, and no one could see what I'd done. From any other angle, it would just look like I was talking to him.

Probably.

Fuck it, the way we conducted our friendship was no one else's business, as I kept reminding myself.

"Thanks. If I lose, do I get a consolation prize?" he

murmured quietly, and I craned my neck to see his face. He looked...amused, almost, and it made me chuckle.

"Course you do. But let's play to win, okay? Team Hammerking."

"Ham—oh, I see what you did there. Combining our usernames. Does that mean that you think you should get half the credit if I win?"

"It's all you, little lion, but I'm still on your team. I'm the support person. It's a very important role."

"Yeah." He smiled again. "Okay. I'll play to win."

I couldn't help ducking my head to press another kiss to his skin, just for luck, you know? That was a thing.

My body tensed when the racers lined up, the teasing and bantering between everyone dying down as the countdown began. Travis and Noah lived together, and Kira was at their house most of the time, so they were all aware of each other's playing styles. Leo was the wild card. I silently willed him on, watching him pull ahead when the players drifted around the first corner of the track, collecting a mushroom boost and timing its use for its best advantage.

In my ideal world, Leo would be wiping the floor with the others, sweeping ahead and winning the whole thing with ease. Unfortunately for us both, we weren't in my ideal world, and by the third lap, he was slightly ahead of Noah when a shell took out his character. Noah raced past him, and then it was all over, Leo screeching into second place just ahead of Kira and Travis.

"I tried." Leo turned to me with a smile. "At least I get a consolation prize."

The way he was looking at me...I couldn't really describe it, but it made my heart beat faster. What did he want his consolation prize to be? My mind was running wild with thoughts I shouldn't be having. Couldn't even believe I was having.

A pair of legs stopped in front of us. "Good game."

After a moment's hesitation, Leo accepted Noah's outstretched hand. "T-thanks. You were really good."

Noah gave him a soft smile, his gaze flicking to me. "You too. Hey, Finn. You should bring your boyfriend over again. It's nice to have some actual competition."

"Boyfriend?" Leo's voice was high and panicked.

I rubbed my thumb over his thigh, reassuring him. "We're friends."

"Oh. Sorry." Noah grimaced. "Shit. I'm really sorry. I shouldn't have assumed..."

"It's okay." *Believe me, you're not the first to think there's something going on between us.* I tried to play it off casually because it was no one else's fucking business. As nice as Noah was, the last thing I wanted was Leo to be stressed and start pulling away from me. "He's just very cuddly. What can I say?"

"Yeah." Noah forced a smile, shifting awkwardly on his feet. "Sorry. Again. I, uh, I'm gonna get a drink. Do either of you want one?"

"We're good, thanks," I said. If Leo wanted a drink, I'd get him one, but I had the feeling that he wanted to be left alone more than anything else.

I was right. As soon as Noah had gone, his shoulders slumped. "Can we go?"

"Yeah, course we can. We'll go now." Everyone was talking among themselves, no one paying us any attention, so now was as good a time as any to leave. As we headed towards the door, I saw JJ watching us, his brows pulled together, but he didn't make a move towards us. I was grateful for that. One confrontation was enough for the night.

By unspoken agreement, we headed back to Leo's flat, both of us lost in our own thoughts. Connor's bedroom door was shut, with a small whiteboard hanging next to it pronouncing that he was doing a Twitch stream and wouldn't be available for the rest of the night. Even so, Leo shut and locked his bedroom door behind us to ensure we wouldn't be disturbed.

"S-sorry." His shoulders hunched over as he stared down at the floor.

There was a heavy weight on my chest. "Leo."

Shaking his head, he turned his back to me, climbing onto his bed and curling into a ball facing the wall. Fuck.

"Leo." I climbed onto the bed next to him, leaning over him in an attempt to see his face. "What's wrong? What do you think you have to be sorry for? Because I can't think of one single thing."

"I'm ruining things for you," he said, and his voice was so small.

What the fuck?

"Ruining what? Baby, please speak to me. I don't understand." It barely even registered that I'd called him "baby"—something I'd never called anyone in my life, but it had just slipped out. I was too worried.

"Things. N-Noah thought we were together, and we're friends, and I'm stopping you from being able to—to get to know people."

My mind raced. He couldn't be saying what I thought he was saying, could he?

"Leo. Please, look at me."

Finally, he turned, and the distraught expression on his face choked me up. It hurt to breathe.

"Leo, I need you to listen to me. Are you saying that you're stopping me from being able to...y'know, hook up with girls?"

He nodded, his lip trembling. "Yeah. If people think we're boyfriends, they won't bother, and—"

"No." I placed a finger to his lips, gently tracing the soft curve of his Cupid's bow. "First of all, I thought we agreed that whether the things we did, like cuddling and whatever might or might not be weird, we didn't care. Second, think about tonight. *I* made a space for you, and *I* was the one to cuddle you...and fuck, to kiss your head or whatever. That was me. Not you. Not like, y'know, I would've done it if I thought you were uncomfortable. The point is, that was all me, and I wanted to do it."

"But what if I'm stopping you from—"

"Leo. You're not stopping me from anything. Believe me, if I wanted to go and flirt with girls, I would. Honestly, though, I'd rather hang out with you over anyone else."

His eyes widened. "But what about y-your needs?" His cheeks flushed redder than I'd ever seen them before, and then he covered his face with his hands. "This is so embarrassing," he mumbled from behind his palms.

"My needs?" I couldn't help smiling. "I have a working right hand."

He groaned. "Finnnn."

"Leooo."

Removing his hands, he glared at me, and it was so much better than him being upset that I had to work to bite back my smile. "Even if I don't feel things the same way as you do, I'm not stupid. We're spending all our free time together, and when we're around people, they apparently think we're boyfriends. So. I'm ruining things for you."

Okay. He needed me to spell it out for him. I manoeuvred him so he was lying flat on his back, and then I propped myself up on my side, cupping his jaw.

"Leo. You're my favourite person in the world. You know that, right?" Fucking hell, this was hard to say. "Sex... yeah, it's fun, but I've never had a high sex drive or anything. Not like, uh, Ander or JJ or someone. I mean, before they were coupled up. I don't wanna think about their sex lives with their boyfriends."

Shaking my head, I tried to get my thoughts back on track. I had to get these words out, to make him understand. "Honestly," I continued, "I can take it or leave it. It's fucking weird for me to be telling you all this, but I'm gonna say it because you need to hear it. *You* are the person I want to spend time with the most. I have everything I need, and for anything else, I have my hand and an active imagination."

He bit down on his lip, and I couldn't help leaning forwards to press a kiss to the freckles on the tip of his nose. If he needed even more reassurance, I'd give it to him.

"If there was someone I was interested in, and right now, there isn't, this wouldn't stop me, so you don't even need to worry about that. You're not an obstacle in the way. You're...Leo. My Leo."

"Oh."

"Is that all you have to say?" My brows rose, and this time, I didn't hide my smile. "I just said all that embarrassing shit to you, and you give me a one-word reply?"

"Shut up," he mumbled, glaring again, and he really was so fucking cute.

"Leoooo."

"Fine. I guess I'll try to believe you. But...will you tell me if I'm too much? Or if...if you want to stop doing what we've been doing?"

I rolled onto my back, pulling him with me. Wrapping my arms around him, I pressed a kiss to his head and then another. Just to emphasise my point. "I'll tell you, but it won't happen. I'm not giving this up for anything and anyone."

He sighed, pressing his face into my throat. A second later, he brushed a soft kiss over my skin.

"Thank you. Sorry I'm...me."

Running a hand up his back and into his hair, I tugged the strands lightly. "Don't ever say that again. You're the best person I know. Now, how about that consolation prize I promised you?"

His head rose, and his eyes met mine, wide and so fucking green. "What's the prize?"

"What do you want?"

He stilled above me, and I could feel his heart pounding just as hard as mine was.

Then, he lowered his head, and our lips met.

FOURTEEN

LEO

"Can we talk?"

I glanced up from my position on the floor where I was stretching out my hamstrings to see JJ giving me a cautious look. We'd just completed an hour's intensive dance training with the other members of our course. Everyone else had left apart from the two of us, and we were both tired out and in need of a shower. But from the way JJ was looking at me, the shower wouldn't be happening just yet.

I nodded in reply to his question, and he sank down next to me, following my moves and beginning a series of leg stretches.

"It's about Finn."

"JJ..."

"Look, I'm not trying to interfere, but you're my friend, and I want to make sure you're okay. You told me about these dares with him, but when we were at the football night, it seemed like there was something more going on with you two. And it's not my place to interfere with your love life, but I...I didn't know. You—" He broke off with a huff of breath. "I'm not explaining myself properly. I guess it just came as a bit of a shock to me. I've known you for almost two years now, and although I don't know Finn very well, you and me are friends."

"You can stop worrying because me and Finn are friends, too."

He stared at me. "Just friends?"

How did I begin to explain our relationship? "Very friendly friends?" I tried.

A tiny smile pulled at his lips. "Okay. Look, you know I'm tactile with a lot of my friends. I've never seen *you* like this before, though."

"You've never seen me with friends, not that I have many," I muttered, and he sighed.

"Leo. You have more friends than you think. Friends that care about you. Hence, me poking my nose into your business."

I let his words sink in for a moment. My shoulders slumped, and I let it all spill out of me. All the things I couldn't make sense of.

"I asked Finn to teach me how to kiss. Dared him, in fact. I, um, there was this girl who seemed interested in me, and I wasn't really interested, but I thought I might be in the future, and I've never kissed anyone before, so I didn't want to make a fool out of myself—"

"Breathe, Leo." JJ shifted closer to me until his shoulder pressed against mine. I looked at him in the mirror that ran from floor to ceiling along one wall of the studio and took a deep breath, exhaling slowly.

"He's never pushed me for anything. We...we're tactile with each other, but it feels nice. How can it be bad if it feels good?"

"It's not bad." JJ's hand covered mine where it was

resting on the floor, and he squeezed lightly. "No one's saying that. You don't owe anyone any explanations, and that includes me. I just wanted to make sure you were okay. I'm looking out for my friend, and that's the only reason I brought it up."

"I know."

"The kissing, then. What happened there?" JJ's voice was lighter, undeniable curiosity in his tone, and I relaxed. It was weird to be talking about this with him, but then, who else could I talk to? Connor wouldn't understand, but maybe JJ would.

"We've kissed a few times. Just practising. It's been... really nice. I like it. You know, I've never really been interested in kissing anyone before, other than feeling like I *should* be interested, but now I can't help wondering if I've been missing out."

"Do you want to kiss anyone else?"

"No," I said immediately.

"But you want to keep kissing Finn."

"Yes." Leaning my head on JJ's shoulder, I sighed. "Is that wrong?"

"It's not wrong, babe. What does Finn think about it all?"

"We spoke about it a bit after the football night, and we agreed we'd tell each other if we wanted to stop anything. I...I think that included the kissing? He seems to be happy with it all."

JJ hummed. "Just make sure you're on the same page. I don't want you to get hurt."

"Okay. I will."

He smiled at me then. "Now I've finished playing the overprotective friend, do you want to get a coffee?"

"Yes! Done!"

I glanced up from my laptop to see Finn staring at his own laptop, a triumphant grin on his face. My breath caught in my throat. The way his eyes were sparkling, the curve of his soft lips against his jaw that had just a hint of stubble darkening it, and his brown hair that was all tousled and messy from him running his hand through it as he worked through the difficult parts of his assignment... It was so nice, seeing him this happy.

When he caught me watching, he ducked his head, still smiling. "That was a bit loud for the library, wasn't it?"

Looking around us, I couldn't see anyone glaring, so he was in the clear. The part of the library we were studying in was quiet, anyway. We'd commandeered a large table next to the windows, and I was working on my group project with Connor and Niall, while Finn had been working on his engineering assignment alongside Bennett, a stack of textbooks piled high between their laptops.

I shook my head. "No one noticed. You finished your assignment?"

"Finished, proofread, and submitted a whole five hours before the deadline."

"Same." Bennett grinned at him triumphantly. "I'm impressed that we finished so early. Why can't this happen every time?"

Next to me, Niall groaned. "I wish we were done with this. Whoever came up with the idea for us to design an entire booking system for a campsite was so deluded. I'm a city boy. I've never even seen a tent in real life."

Connor snorted. "The camping bit isn't the important part. It's the programming and the databases and all that.

We're the tech guys. We make things work so other people can go camping."

"Yeah, but I'm just saying, it would've been better to design a booking system for something we were familiar with..."

I tuned them out as they continued their bickering, my gaze returning to Finn, who was now frowning down at his phone.

"Finn?"

He blinked, and then he held out his phone to me, the screen angled so I could read the text.

CHARLIE:

Friday night. Student union. Bring Leo. There's a DJ set and they're doing BOGOF drinks. All the girls will be there

Friday. Crowds. Drinking. Girls.

I bit down on my lip.

Finn glanced at Bennett, who was engrossed in his own phone, before turning back to me. Shifting his chair closer to mine, he lowered his voice. "Don't feel like you have to say yes. No one's forcing you to go. We don't have to do anything. I thought it might be a good way to celebrate after getting our assignments finished, but you know I'm just as happy doing our own thing."

This wouldn't be like the club, where there was a smaller group of us and we were anonymous in the crowd. Nor would it be like the casual atmosphere of the football night at Travis' house—and even then, I'd ended up in my head, worried that I was ruining things for Finn. Despite the assurances he'd given me, there was still doubt in my mind that he really meant it.

Maybe the best thing to do was to persuade him to go

alone. Then I wouldn't have to feel guilty about holding him back, and I wouldn't have to face my fear of going out and being surrounded by so many of my peers.

Dropping my gaze to my laptop, I hit a few random keys. "I... No. I can't go. I have too much coursework to do. You should, though. It sounds like fun."

"Leo. I want you to come. If you want to, that is."

I couldn't hold him back. I wouldn't allow him to put me before himself. I needed to persuade him to go and that I'd be fine without him. Because I *would*. "It's okay. I need to get my work finished. You can tell me all about it on Saturday. I-I'll come over, and if you're hungover, we can laze around in your bedroom and have a gaming day."

"Are you sure?"

"Yeah. I'm sure. You should go." If I said it enough times, I'd convince myself I meant it. And I didn't want him to turn down invitations because of me, anyway. That was so wrong.

He sighed. "Okay. But if you want me to come over or anything instead, you know I will."

"I won't, but thanks. I'll be fine."

"Okay. If you're sure." Finally, his doubtful look was gone, and his bright smile was back. And really, that was all I wanted.

FIFTEEN

LEO

"Hi, Dad."

"Leo?" The surprise in my dad's voice was clear over the sounds of talking and glasses clinking in the background. "What's wrong?"

"Um. Nothing. I just wanted to say hi." Lying on my bed, I'd been scrolling through my phone as I attempted to take my mind off the fact that I hadn't gone to the student union—that I'd just turned it down for no other reason than my fears. Fear of holding Finn back and fear of being in a social situation. It was then that I realised I hadn't spoken to my dad in over a month. According to my call log, I'd made six attempts to call him over the past four weeks, and I knew I'd left at least three voicemails, but the only correspondence we'd had were a few sporadic texts where he'd wished me luck in my assignments, and I'd replied.

The background noise suddenly cut out with the slam of a door, and my dad spoke again. "It's a Friday night. Shouldn't you be out with your friends?"

"I didn't really feel like it. I'm having a quiet night in."

He huffed through the phone. "Leo. What's that attitude all about? Even I'm out with my friends. You should be out having fun and enjoying your student years, not shut up in your bedroom staring at a collection of pixels. It's not healthy. I've told you this before."

"Yeah. Um. I went out to a club the other day."

"Now, that's more like it. How's uni going? Met any nice girls yet?"

"I've met a nice boy," I said without thinking. There was a long pause, and I realised how that had sounded. "Not like that. I mean, I made a new friend."

My dad laughed. "However you meant it, it's good news. Means you're out socialising instead of hiding yourself away. But, Leo, making a new friend or even a partner shouldn't be something you have to tell me, not at your age. You're a grown man, and you've been at that uni for nearly two years. What are you doing with yourself?"

I swallowed hard. "Well. Uh, I got my dance module results back. They—"

"Tell me about your computing project, the one you were doing with the...what did you say in the text? A booking system? That's something useful, a real skill you can build on. If you want me to use my contacts, put some feelers out for your future employment, you know I will. Just say the word."

"Thanks."

"Right. I've got to go. The pub quiz is about to start. Why don't you call this new 'friend' and get yourself down to the pub, eh? I'll talk to you soon. Take care, alright?"

The call cut out, and I threw my phone down next to me, letting my eyes close as I focused on taking deep, calming breaths. I knew my dad was just trying to be helpful, and I knew he struggled because he felt like he couldn't relate to me, but it didn't stop it hurting.

My phone vibrated softly with a text alert.

FINN:

Wish you were here. I hope you're not
working too hard

My dad's words flashed through my mind.

*It's a Friday night. Shouldn't you be out with your
friends? You should be out having fun and enjoying your
student years, not shut up in your bedroom staring at a
collection of pixels. Why don't you call this new "friend" and
get yourself down to the pub, eh?*

Another message came through.

FINN:

Not trying to guilt trip you! Just saying I
wish you were here. Looking forward to a
whole day of gaming tomorrow

Fuck. Resigned, I climbed off my bed and pulled on the
hoodie that was draped over the back of my gaming chair.

***

Steeling myself, I entered the student union, immediately
accosted by a wall of noise and the smell of stale alcohol and
too much perfume and aftershave in the air.

I sucked in a shaky breath as I hugged the wall, moving
in the direction of the bar. *No one's looking at you, Leo.* If I
kept repeating it to myself, I might believe it.

Rationally, I knew no one was actually paying me any
attention, too focused on themselves or whoever they were
here with, but my brain was anything but rational. I could
swear I felt hundreds of eyes on me, but every time I looked
around, no one was watching me.

Eventually, though, I made it to the bar without incident. A tiny smile tugged at my lips as I leaned against the counter. I'd done it. I was here, at the student union, all on my own, and—oh, now I had to speak to someone so I could order a drink.

Gripping the pitted wooden counter, slightly sticky beneath my fingers, I swallowed hard.

"Leo!"

My head shot up, and I was confronted by the sight of Charlie grinning at me from behind the bar. I frowned, my nerves momentarily forgotten.

"What are you doing here?"

He laughed. "Working, obviously."

"Yeah, but I mean, aren't you supposed to be meeting Finn and the—the girls?"

"After my shift. I wasn't supposed to be working at all tonight, but they asked me to cover the first hour of someone else's shift because they couldn't make it in time, and I couldn't turn down the extra money. I've only got another fifteen minutes left, then I'll join them."

Oh. That made sense. "I didn't know you worked here," I said.

"I guess it never came up." He shrugged. "Want a drink? I'll give you mates' rates."

"Please. Uhh." I stared at the taps and then at the rows of bottles behind Charlie.

"Vodka and Coke? A little caffeine buzz for energy and a hit of alcohol to give it a punch?"

"Okay. Yeah. Thanks."

Shooting me a grin, he grabbed a glass and added the vodka and Coke along with a generous helping of ice. Sliding it across the bar, he nodded towards the card machine.

I unlocked my phone and held it to the reader. When the payment confirmation showed up, I realised he'd only charged me a pound. My gaze flew to his, but before I could say anything, he held a finger to his lips.

"Mates' rates, remember? It's good to see you here. Go and find your boy and let him know I'm on my way."

"M-my boy?"

Charlie laughed at whatever my face was doing. "Yeah. Finn. You know him? Plays football. So high." He held his hand in the air. "Normally seen joined at the hip with a certain redhead."

My face was on fire. A sound came out of my mouth that was definitely not a squeak, and I escaped the bar as fast as I could. Whether Charlie had meant something innocent with that comment or not, it brought all my insecurities flooding back. Fuck. What was I even doing here?

You're here to prove a point to yourself. And to see Finn.

This talking to myself in my head was getting old, fast.

I sipped my drink as I made my way through the student union, scanning the faces I passed to see if I could spot Finn anywhere. Even though I was second-guessing myself, I was determined to see this through. After about five minutes of circling, my nerves were a little more settled. I still hadn't seen Finn, but I'd managed to convince myself that people really weren't looking at me.

Smiling down at my drink, I ran straight into a wall.

"Watch it, dickhead!"

Two things registered instantly. I hadn't run into a wall but a person—a huge man, to be precise—who was now glaring at me. And my entire front was now soaked with beer.

"I-I-I'm sorry," I burst out.

"Y-y-you fucking better be," he sneered, mimicking my

stutter with a curl of his lip. My stomach clenched, and I begged my body to not react outwardly, even as my lip trembled. "You spilled my entire fucking pint. What are you gonna do about it?"

"I-I'll pay for a new one," I gasped out, stumbling backwards as he loomed over me. "It was—it was an accident."

Crowding up against my back, he followed me all the way to the bar, where he ordered another drink, and I paid for it with shaking hands. I would've given anything to see Charlie there, to have a friendly face in my vicinity, but he was gone.

The guy left after muttering something uncomplimentary about me that I really wished I hadn't heard, and I made a beeline for the toilet block. Locked inside one of the stalls, I pressed my forehead against the door, closing my eyes and trying to breathe. I bit down on my lip so hard I tasted blood, but despite my best efforts, a tiny sob fell from my throat when I opened my mouth. Rubbing the wetness away from my eyes, I counted under my breath until my breathing was under control. Why couldn't I be normal? Why did I have to fuck up so much?

I needed Finn. I didn't care if it made me weak or needy or whatever; I just wanted him to wrap me in his arms and tell me everything was okay. Blindly, I stumbled out of the stall and made my way back into the student union, desperately scanning the crowds. My vision was blurred from the tears that wouldn't stop forming despite my best efforts, and I rubbed my face with my hoodie sleeve, still wet from the drink that had spilled over me, before pulling my hood up over my head. Maybe it looked weird for me to have my hood up inside, but at least it would help to hide the fact that I'd been crying.

My heart was pounding, and my breaths were fast and

shallow as I entered the part of the student union where the DJ booth was set up. The music was so much louder in here, the bass throbbing in time with my elevated heart rate, but it was a relief in a way because it gave me something else to focus on.

Lights swept across the packed dance floor, and then I saw Finn.

Leaning down to a girl I didn't recognise, a familiar grin on his face, the one that came so easily to him, he looked completely at ease. He looked happy. As I stood, frozen in place, I watched him shake his head, his grin widening as the girl went up on her toes to say something into his ear, his hand casually landing on her waist to hold her in place while she spoke. My stomach churned, and as I tore my gaze away, I noticed Charlie next to them with his arm draped over Sophie's shoulders. It took me a second to realise that Charlie wasn't the only other one there—there was a whole group of LSU footballers and their friends and partners. Every one of them seemed confident and happy, enjoying their Friday night.

Like normal people do.

What was I doing? I shouldn't have come here. If I went over there, Finn would feel obligated to speak to me, maybe even leave, and he was clearly having fun. I was all wrong for him. He deserved better than a stupid, clingy boy who was hopeless at interacting socially and couldn't even fucking handle walking through the student union without messing up.

Tears filled my eyes again, and this time, I didn't bother to brush them away. The only thought left in my head was that I had to get out of there before Finn saw me. I pushed through the crowds, mumbling apologies, receiving a sharp elbow to the ribs that made me gasp as the breath was punched out of me, but I didn't stop. By the time I hit the bar area, I was running, swerving around people in my haste to get away. My rib was hurting from the elbow jab I'd received, my eyes were stinging, and I wasn't paying enough attention to my surroundings.

"You again! Get out of my fucking way!" a voice snarled, and before I could register what was happening, I was being shoved, hard, and then I was falling backwards, hitting the wall with a thud. I crumpled to the floor, the cold surface tacky with spilled drinks.

Curling my body over, I made myself as small as possible.

"...probably drunk..."

"Did you see the way he was running?"

"...knobhead..."

"...already wasted, and it's not even nine o'clock..."

The sobs tore from my throat unchecked. I couldn't have stopped them if I'd tried. My breaths were coming so fast and shallow that I was light-headed.

I wrapped my arms around myself, my body trembling as I struggled to remember how to breathe.

"Leo? Leo?" A hand touched my shoulder, and I flinched. "Leo. It's Nic. Are you okay? What am I saying? Of course you're not." The voice seemed to be coming from a great distance away, even though I could feel the hand on my arm and the heat of a body next to mine. I curled into myself even further, trying to make myself invisible as all around me, the whispers continued.

I was falling apart, and everyone was looking at me. Judging me.

An anguished sound ripped out of me, a sound I didn't even know I could make, and Niccolò swore. Through the haze, I caught snatches of him saying words, words that refused to register in my brain. I didn't know how long I remained there, trembling and trying to breathe through my sobs, but suddenly, the pressure of his hand was gone, almost instantly replaced by another. Two hands, this time, firmly gripping my shoulders.

"Leo. Take a breath. Like we do in dance. In, then out. With me." I concentrated on the voice patiently repeating the instructions to me until I finally managed to take a deep, shuddering breath.

"Good. And again," he said, and I breathed again, and then again, until the pressure in my chest lessened, and then, even though I didn't want to, I opened my swollen eyes.

"Oh, babe," JJ said sadly. "Come on. Do you think you can stand? Let's get you out of here."

Niccolò appeared in my field of vision, silently pulling my fallen hood back over my head. Together, the two of them helped me stand, JJ holding on to me and Niccolò doing his best to shield me with his body as we left the student union.

"My house is closest," JJ murmured to Niccolò, steering me to the right. I drifted, letting him guide me wherever he wanted, too drained to think about where we were going and what we were doing.

The cooler air was replaced with warmth, and then there were stairs that seemed never-ending, but finally, there was a soft bed, and I was being carefully pushed down onto it.

"His hoodie's all wet. Looks like someone threw a whole pint onto it," Niccolò whispered.

"Yeah. Hey, Leo? Lift your arms, babe. We're gonna get you out of these wet clothes, okay?"

I lifted my arms, hissing in pain when JJ brushed over the spot on my rib where I'd been elbowed.

"Leo? What is it?"

I licked my cracked lips and then attempted a reply, my voice coming out hoarse and broken. "Elbow. Ribs."

"Those fuckers! I'll chop their dicks off if they do that again," Niccolò vowed, and somehow, I found myself almost smiling at his deadly serious tone.

"I'll get some ice. Nic, get Leo a hoodie. The zip one over there by the window."

I closed my eyes, not bothering to open them again while a clean hoodie was gently pulled over my shoulders and zipped up, and then a bag of something cold was pressed onto my ribs, right where it hurt. I let my head sink into the pillows, concentrating on breathing slowly and evenly.

The bed dipped next to me, and when I opened my eyes again, JJ was lying next to me, his hand rubbing up and down my arm. On my other side, Niccolò laid his head on my chest, keeping well away from my bruised rib, his body curling into mine. Like this, with their warm, comforting presence blanketing me, I felt like I could finally breathe properly.

"Do you want to talk about it?" JJ asked.

"Not really. But I guess I should." Before either of them could respond, I began to talk, the words spilling out of me. I shared my conversation with my dad, and my decision to go out tonight and find Finn, and everything that had happened. By the time I finished, my face was wet with tears, my voice was raw, and JJ and Niccolò were both cuddling into me, comforting me in the best way they knew.

"You know you're my friend, right?" Nic said quietly. "I

know we haven't spoken much, but I like you, Leo. And you know what? I love going out and partying, and I can be loud and dramatic and—"

"My little drama queen," JJ interrupted, giving Nic a fond smile.

Niccolò grinned at him and then continued. "My point is, I like all those things, but I don't need all my friends to like everything I do or have the same personality as me. My boyfriend isn't really a big partier, and JJ's really, really isn't. I mean, Daddy K would probably rather poke his own eyeballs out than be seen in the student union."

"Where all his students are," JJ interjected. "But he's right. Boyfriends, friends, whatever—we don't need to share all the same interests. I'm all for you pushing yourself out of your comfort zone, babe, because you're capable of a lot more than you think, but not if it upsets you the way it did tonight."

My lip trembled. "It's my brain. It convinces me that there's something wrong with me or that e-everyone's staring at me and thinking horrible things. And then I saw Finn looking so happy, and then—" My breath hitched, and useless tears filled my eyes again. I was so fucking sick of crying. "Then I heard what people were saying about me when I got pushed over."

Niccolò muttered something in Italian that I didn't understand, but from the murderous look on his face, I was guessing it wasn't complimentary.

"I'm sorry," I said in a small voice. "Sorry you had to cut your night short to babysit m—"

JJ covered my mouth. "Stop. You have nothing to be sorry for, and we're not babysitting you. You're our friend, and we want to spend time with you. Imagine it was me in your situation. Would you leave me there on my own when I was clearly as upset as you were?"

Slowly, I shook my head. Not that JJ would ever be in my situation—or so I hoped—but I would never dream of leaving him if he was.

"I think speaking to my dad earlier just triggered me. And you know I find it hard to be normal."

"Normal doesn't exist," said JJ.

"Normal is boring," announced Nic at exactly the same time. They looked at each other and laughed, lightening the heavy atmosphere.

I sighed. "Thank you. Both of you. You...you don't know how much this means to me."

Niccolò bit down on his lip. "We're not the only ones who are here for you. I think...I think if Finn had known about all this, he'd be here right now."

I shrugged, and he shook his head insistently. "Bennett says he talks about you a lot. He just drops you into most of his conversations without even realising he's doing it."

He did?

"Oh. Uh. Yeah, I don't really think he needs to be bothered with all this, not while he's out having fun after working so hard all week."

JJ eyed me thoughtfully but didn't comment, and after a few seconds of silence, Niccolò grabbed my hand, launching himself into a seated position.

"Enough moping. We're gonna salvage the rest of this night." He batted his lashes at me. "Leo, please will you teach me how to play *Mario Kart* so I can surprise my boyfriend by beating him?"

"Okay." I climbed off the bed after him. This was what I needed. Something to take my mind off everything that had happened tonight.

And if I wished more than anything that Finn were there to wrap me up and tell me everything would be okay... that was best kept to myself.

SIXTEEN

FINN

I stared at the text with dawning horror. "I have to go," I said, cutting off Charlie mid-sentence.

"Everything okay?" he asked, but I didn't have time to talk. There was only one thing I needed to do, and that was to get to number 1, the Mansions.

Leo was hurting, and I hadn't been there for him.

By the time I reached the Victorian terrace where JJ lived with his housemates, I was panting, out of breath from my sprint there. Before I could knock, the door swung open, and JJ was standing there, blocking my path to Leo, his arms folded across his chest.

"Before I let you in, I want to say something. Whatever this is between you and Leo isn't my business. What *is* my business is my friend's happiness. You fuck with him, and you'll live to regret it." I'd never seen him act so cold before. JJ was warm, social, the life of the party. But right now, he was looking at me as if he'd happily slit my throat if I made the wrong move.

"I understand. I don't want to hurt him. Ever. I'd never purposely make him upset. He...he's the most important person in the world to me," I said, and fucking hell, my voice was cracking.

JJ's expression softened slightly, but he still didn't move. "He told me about the kissing for practice. What are you getting out of it? I don't want you to take advantage of him. He's not...experienced."

"And he knows his own fucking mind," I ground out, trying to keep my cool. "I'd never take advantage of him."

"Answer my question."

Question... Oh, fuck. How was I supposed to answer that? "Uh...I like it, okay? What business is it of yours?"

"You like kissing Leo," JJ stated. The corners of his lips turned up, and I wasn't sure I liked the expression on his face.

"That's what I fucking said. Are you gonna let me in after panicking me with your text, or do I have to stand out here all night?"

"One more thing, and I'll let you in. Two things, in fact. Be patient with him. It might take a while for you both to be on the same page. And the other thing." He paused until I raised my brows, impatiently gesturing with my hands for him to continue. Now, he smiled properly. No, it was a smirk. "Think about why you like kissing him."

"Whatever," I mumbled, pushing past him into the hallway when he finally stepped aside. He stopped me with a hand on my arm.

"I'm serious."

Scrubbing my hand across my face, I nodded. "I know you are. I just...I really need to see him."

"Okay. He's in the lounge with Nic, playing *Mario Kart*."

"Thanks."

I barely noticed JJ following me into the lounge and Niccolò quickly ending the game, both of them discreetly exiting the room. I only had eyes for Leo, curled up in the corner of the sofa wearing someone else's hoodie, his eyes all red and swollen and his soft lips cracked and bitten. It hurt so much to see him like that, and I didn't even know what had happened to make him so upset. All I knew was that JJ had told me that Leo had a really upsetting evening and needed me now.

"Leo. Baby," I choked out, and his head flew up, his eyes wide as he stared at me. Reaching the sofa, I wasted no time in sinking into it and pulling him into my arms. He winced, and I immediately stilled, but then he burrowed into me, wrapping his arms around my neck and pressing his nose into my throat.

"Finn," he breathed shakily, overwhelming relief in his voice, and I simultaneously felt like crying and fucking killing anyone who'd contributed to my best friend being in such a state.

I held on to him, gently rubbing up and down his back and pressing soft kisses to the parts of his head I could reach. When he eventually sat up straight, he looked at me with huge, sad eyes, his bottom lip trembling. Fucking hell, it was agonising seeing him like this. I'd do anything to take his pain away.

"What happened?" I said, leaning forwards to kiss his cheek. "Please tell me."

He made a whimpering sound and buried his face in the juncture of my neck and shoulder again. Eventually, the whole story came out, and by the end, he wasn't the only one with tears in his eyes. I wished more than anything that I could have done things differently, but I couldn't. All I could do was be there for him now and to let him know I wasn't going anywhere. I needed to thank JJ and Niccolò, too. If they hadn't been there...

The thought of him all alone, crying on the floor, *killed* me.

"I'm so sorry, baby," I murmured, stroking my thumb gently under his eyes, brushing his tears away. I couldn't give a single fuck about the fact that I was still calling him "baby" and that JJ and Niccolò were probably spying on us and would hear me and probably see that I couldn't stop kissing him. All I wanted to do was to make him happy again.

"Not your fault," he mumbled, curling back into me. A yawn overtook him. "Sorry. I'm so tired."

"Yeah, I can see that. I'm not surprised. Want me to take you home? Mine or yours?"

He nodded. "Yours, please."

I helped him upright, and he eased the bag of frozen peas out from under his hoodie, placing them on the coffee table.

"How are your ribs?"

"They're okay. I'll be fine tomorrow. It wasn't a hard jab. I think they just caught me at a bad angle."

My jaw clenched at the way he tried to brush off the fact that someone had purposely hurt him. And the bastard who had pushed him...if I ever found out who it was, he'd have not only me but the entire football team to deal with, not to mention JJ and Niccolò.

"Leo."

"Don't. Please."

"It's okay." I kissed his temple. "We don't have to talk about it anymore if you don't want to."

"I don't want to. I just want to go home with you."

How could I ever refuse him anything when he gave me

that imploring look? There was one thing I needed to do first, though. Unzipping the hoodie and easing it off his shoulders, I then removed my own hoodie. I carefully helped him into it, reluctantly smiling when he stared at me, his brows rising in an unspoken question.

A question I didn't really have the answer to. "It makes sense for you to wear my hoodie, otherwise you'll have to remember to give this one back to..."

"JJ," he finished.

"Right. JJ. Now you can wear mine, and we can take yours home to wash."

He smiled then, a proper, genuine smile, and my breath caught in my throat. Fucking hell.

"Okay. Let's get home," I said hoarsely, pulling him upright. As we left the lounge, Leo's hand clasped securely in mine, we ran into JJ.

"Nice hoodie," he murmured, amused, his gaze flicking between us. Leaning into me, he lowered his voice. "Remember what I said earlier."

I glared at him, and he smirked, but his expression became serious as he turned to Leo.

"If you need anything, just text me, okay? Anything at all."

"Same goes for me," Niccolò called from the kitchen, where he'd obviously been eavesdropping.

"Thank you," Leo whispered.

"Anytime." JJ pulled him into a one-armed hug, giving the side of his head a quick kiss, amusement dancing in his eyes when he noticed the way I was staring at him. Not that I was looking at him in a certain kind of way. I just had a bit of tension in my jaw, that was all.

I forced myself to concentrate on the fact that JJ and Niccolò had been really good friends to Leo tonight. They'd both done everything they could to make sure he was okay, and I was seriously grateful to them both. JJ didn't have to text me, either, but he had, and I needed to thank him.

"Thanks for texting me," I said quietly, meeting JJ's gaze. "It means a lot."

He nodded to acknowledge me, giving me a brief but genuine smile. "Look after him, okay?"

"I will." It was a promise I'd do everything I could to keep.

Back at my house, I sorted Leo out with some soft, loose joggers and a faded T-shirt to wear to bed. I left him to get ready, heading for the kitchen to fill a glass with water from the fridge while I waited to get into the bathroom to dig out the paracetamol, lip balm, and my mum's eye cream. I knew she wouldn't mind me using it for a good cause.

When I returned from the bathroom, Leo was in my bed, propped up by one of my pillows.

I placed the water on my bedside table and handed him the paracetamol. "Take two of these. I'm just gonna get changed, then I'll be back."

He nodded to acknowledge me, and I quickly ducked into the bathroom to get ready for bed. As soon as I was done, I got Leo to close his eyes while I carefully applied the cream, followed by a generous coating of lip balm, which I hoped would make his lips less sore. When I was done, I turned off the lights, leaving my curtains open a sliver, as usual, in case he needed to get up in the night.

"Thanks, Finn. I-I'm sorry—"

Climbing into bed next to him and sliding under the covers, I shook my head. "I don't want to hear you apologising to me again unless it's something you actually need to apologise for, which I doubt will ever happen."

He sighed but fell silent. We both lay on our backs, staring up at the dark ceiling.

"*I'm* sorry. I wish I'd been there."

Leo inhaled sharply, and then he shifted over, nudging under my arm until I had it curved around him and his arm was slung across my waist.

"You don't need to be sorry, either. I don't want to be dependent on you or anyone." He stretched to kiss my jaw. The light touch gave me a shiver. "I'm glad we're here now, though."

"Me too," I said, closing my eyes and allowing sleep to drag me under.

SEVENTEEN

FINN

When I made it downstairs in the morning, Leo was standing at the kitchen counter wearing a pair of my joggers and one of my hoodies, his hair damp from the shower, pouring water from the kettle into a collection of mugs while my mum buttered thick slices of toast.

"...No, it doesn't really hurt anymore. It was only a brief jab. Finn did a good job of looking after me."

I froze in the doorway. Leo was voluntarily telling my mum about last night? Why did that realisation bring a lump to my throat?

"He's a good boy." My mum smiled. "I think you should have two more paracetamols with your breakfast, even so. I want you to take care of yourself, love. No more putting yourself into situations where you could get hurt, okay? If you need a quiet place to go, you know our home is yours, whether Finn's here or not."

Placing the kettle down, Leo stared at her, wide-eyed. "Um." He licked his lips. "I will. Thanks." I thought he was going to stop there, but he carried on speaking, his voice growing soft and impossibly sad. "I wish...I wish my dad understood me like you do." His lip wobbled, and I went to rush forwards, but my mum got there first, dropping the butter knife and wrapping her arms around him. I could see his body tremble, and it took everything in me to hold myself in place, but this wasn't a moment for me to interrupt.

When they drew apart, I could see the glistening tracks of tears on Leo's cheeks.

"I-I've never had a hug from a mum before. Not since I was a baby, and I can't remember that."

Fucking *hell*. I couldn't stay where I was any longer. As I barrelled into him, I saw my mum turn, discreetly wiping away her own tears. I glanced at her over Leo's shoulder, holding out my arm, and she took the invitation. I hugged them both, so fucking grateful that I had a family who had made Leo feel so welcome, to the point where he wasn't afraid to share the important things with them.

"Well..." My mum dabbed at her eyes again before giving me a tremulous smile. "I don't know about you boys, but I think this situation calls for a nice cup of tea. Finn, do you want to grab the milk and help Leo finish making it while I get this toast buttered?"

I nodded, releasing Leo after kissing his temple. As I moved towards the fridge, I noticed my brother hovering in the doorway, shifting from foot to foot. He must've been standing right behind me, and I wondered how much he'd overheard. He glanced at me, then at Leo, then at my mum, and finally, back at Leo. Squaring his shoulders, he walked into the kitchen, straight up to Leo, who was fishing teabags out of the mugs, and threw his arms around him from behind. Leo startled, sending the teabag on his spoon to the counter with a wet splat, but he recovered quickly, his lips curving upwards as he squeezed Ed's arm.

Ed went to move away, but he didn't get very far. My mum grabbed him, hugging him and leaning up to whisper something in his ear, which made him give her an uncharacteristically shy smile. Okay, so that was probably my cue as his big brother. Grabbing the milk from the fridge, I detoured to Leo, placing the bottle on the counter next to the mugs, and then moved around him to dip my head to Ed's ear.

"Thanks," was all I said, but the word was loaded with meaning, and I knew my brother understood because he shot me a bright grin. In what I assumed was an effort to lighten the emotional atmosphere, he flipped the radio on, and we got the tea and toast set up at the kitchen table while Capital FM played in the background. My dad wandered into the kitchen, swiping a piece of toast from the pile and giving my mum a loud, smacking kiss when she told him off. She shook her head at him, Ed absorbed himself in his phone while he shovelled toast into his mouth, and Leo kept looking down at the table, smiling to himself in between sips of tea and bites of toast.

It was one of the best mornings I'd had in a long time. And I was pretty sure it was the same for Leo.

"One more game? Then we should take a break."

I nodded, my attention focused on the screen as I watched the numbers increasing, a shower of sparks confirming that my character had levelled up. We'd been playing *Lesath Legends* all day, with a quick break for lunch, but it would probably do our eyes good to have another break. The house was silent—Ed was out with his friends, and my parents had gone to an art exhibition somewhere in

London and then out for a meal afterwards. We had the house to ourselves, and I had a bit of an idea of what I'd like to do during our next break, if Leo was on the same page.

"Want to do the double loot challenge?" I suggested, scrolling through the list. "It's only ten minutes."

Instead of replying to me, Leo slid off the bed, leaving his controller behind. I stared at him, my brows raised as he came around to my chair and leaned back against my desk.

"Hi," I said.

"Hi. Want to do a dare?"

I grinned. "Hmm. I dunno. What's the dare? I was actually gonna suggest we do dares for our break because I haven't dared you to do anything for a while."

"Well... We could take a break now before we start the next challenge." Leo's eyes sparkled. I was suddenly struck by the fact that he was so fucking pretty. That was definitely a weird thing for me to be thinking about him, but it was true. There was all that red hair falling into his sparkly green eyes and that mouth that, thanks to my efforts with the lip balm, was now all soft-looking again. The mouth that was currently curved into a mischievous smile directed at me.

I placed down my controller and rolled my chair forwards so my calves were touching his. "And what's the dare...?"

He leaned down, placing his hands on the arms of my chair. I only caught a second of his expression of shock before the chair rolled backwards, Leo collapsing into me as laughter burst from my throat.

"Smooth, Leo," I said between laughter. He straddled my thighs, glaring at me.

"I can't believe you're laughing at my misfortune."

"Aww. Sorry, baby." I pulled him into me, dragging my nose up the side of his face. The familiar scent of apple pie hit me. "Hey, you used my shampoo."

"Was that not allowed?"

"Yeah, course it's allowed. It smells nice on you."

"I guess you're the hair sniffer now," he said, taking me back to a conversation we'd had a while ago.

"That means you have to kiss me to make it even in the weirdness department. That's what I did to you last time, wasn't it?"

He nodded against me, and then he turned his head, brushing a soft kiss over my cheek.

"Finn?"

"Yeah?"

"Why...uh...why are you calling me baby?"

Good question.

"I dunno. It just seems to happen. Do you not like it? I can stop."

"No, I like it," he whispered into my ear, like he was confiding a secret. "You just have all these nicknames for me, like baby and little lion and Viking, and I don't have any for you."

"Hmm." I ran my hand down his back. "I'd prefer not to be known as Hammerhead outside of our games. Definitely not Sharkfin. It's bad enough when Ed calls me that. Honestly, I'm good with you just calling me by my name. I'm not really a nickname person."

I felt him smile against me. "Okay, Finn. Want to do a dare?"

"Yeah. What do you have in mind?"

"I dare you to play the next campaign against me. One v one, instead of as a team."

"It's a dare," I said immediately. "Does the winner get a reward?"

"Bragging rights? The in-game loot?"

"Not good enough. I think the winner should get to pick the takeaway we order for dinner. How about it?"

Drawing back, he nodded. He climbed off me and settled back on the bed while I wheeled my chair into place. "Okay. Let's go."

It was close, as it always was, because we were so evenly matched. We rarely played against each other, preferring to work as a team, but our competitive streaks definitely came out when we played against each other. When there were just thirty seconds left on the timer and our scores were still even, I decided to try a dirty trick. Holding my controller with one hand, I reached out and tickled the underside of Leo's foot. He shrieked at an ear-splitting volume, jumping away from me, and it only took me a few seconds of him being distracted to rack up the extra points I needed to win the game.

"You cheat!" he shouted, throwing his controller down and launching himself at me. I was weak with laughter from the utter outrage on his face, and I couldn't have stopped his onslaught if I'd tried. His momentum was so strong that the entire chair tipped backwards, sending us crashing to the carpet.

"Fucking hell, Leo," I wheezed, rolling away from the chair and collapsing onto my back. I couldn't breathe through my laughter.

"Cheating bastard." He threw himself onto my torso, knocking what remained of my breath out of me. I brought my hands up to hold him in place, and he stilled. I ran a soothing hand down his spine.

"I'm sorry. I just couldn't resist."

"You're not sorry," he muttered, his outraged glare replaced by a cute little pout, which made me grin.

"Okay, I'm not sorry. What can I say? I was just really in the mood for fried chicken tonight, and I knew you'd pick pizza."

"I wouldn't," he lied.

"Leo."

He huffed loudly. "I hate you."

"Two lies in a row. I can't believe you." Shifting him off me, I climbed to my feet and righted my gaming chair, pushing it back into place. I really needed to look into buying something a little more stable. Without wheels.

"I wasn't lying."

I shook my head, tutting. "Three lies in a row." Biting back a grin, I placed our controllers next to the console and then lay back on my bed.

"I may be a liar, but you're a dirty cheat." Leo crawled over me, like I was hoping he'd do, holding himself up in a plank position. I sometimes forgot how strong his core actually was, what with all his dance training, and then he'd do something like this, which would surprise me all over again.

"We make a good pair, then, don't we?" My gaze flicked to his mouth.

His tongue swiped across his lips, and his lashes lowered. "Yeah."

"Yeah," I repeated, curving my hand around the back of his neck and pulling him down to me. He came willingly, sliding his mouth across mine without hesitation.

It was so fucking perfect. How could he kiss so well? I found my arms sliding down his back and then around to his sides, pulling him fully on top of me as we deepened the kiss, and—

Oh. *Fuck.*

My dick was hard, right against him, and he was going to be aware of it any second—

A soft whine fell from his lips, swallowed by my mouth, as he ground down, his hard dick pressing against mine.

Wait a fucking minute.

Leo's. Hard. Dick.

Leo Evans was on top of me, and he was hard.

Holy fuck.

I had *no idea* what to do except to kiss him back, holding on to him, and brace myself for the second he realised what was happening and the moment came crashing to a halt.

Except he made that soft noise again, which sent a shudder through my body, and he kissed me even harder, his body pressing down more insistently on mine.

It was *so fucking good.*

I hated myself for what I had to do.

EIGHTEEN

FINN

"Leo," I mumbled against his lips. "Leo."

"Mmm?" He blinked down at me, all flushed cheeks, blown pupils, and kiss-swollen lips. Fucking gorgeous.

"We should stop."

His body froze, hurt flashing in his gaze. Without a word, he rolled off me, onto his side, facing the wall.

"Fuck. No. That's not what I meant." Collapsing onto my back, I rubbed my hand over my face, attempting to gather myself. When I'd managed to catch my breath and my dick was no longer threatening to punch a hole through my joggers, I shifted onto my side, pressing my chest up against Leo's back, although I kept my hips angled away from him. I didn't trust my dick to behave, and holy fuck, Leo Evans made my dick hard. Okay, maybe I'd known that for a while, but it was something I'd been hoping would go away. Leo was my best friend, and the only reason we'd even started this whole kissing thing in the first place was to help him practise. And okay, maybe now we just kissed because we both liked it or whatever, but—

A tiny whimper came from Leo, and I reacted instantly, gripping his arm and turning him onto his back. He covered his face with his hands, his knees drawn up, and he looked so vulnerable. I couldn't stand it. I had to make this right.

"Leo. Baby. Look at me."

He shook his head violently. Propping myself up on one elbow, I leaned down to kiss the back of his hand.

"Please."

Another head shake. I sighed.

"I didn't want to stop. I just—I was worried you—*we* were getting carried away. Y'know, with, uh, you know." Fuck me, this was a hard conversation to have.

"You really didn't want to stop?" His voice came out muffled, but I heard the uncertainty in his tone.

"Really. I think you could tell I was into it."

Slowly, he lowered his hands. He still wouldn't look at me, but it was a start. "I was into it, too, so I don't understand."

Fuck. He sounded so confused and hurt. I was really going to have to spell it out, wasn't I? "Leo. We were grinding on each other. Kissing is one thing, but we've never discussed taking it further, and I didn't want to get carried away and have you regret it, you know?" My face was on *fire*. Believe me, this was not a discussion I'd ever envisioned.

I could practically see the wheels turning in his head. There was a moment where he paused, and then... Swiping his tongue across his lips, he met my gaze directly, his eyes widening, and the last thing I expected happened.

He lowered his legs, arched a brow, and said, "Are you saying *you* wouldn't have regretted it?"

"Uh—well—uh—no. No, I wouldn't."

"Neither would I." Lifting his hand, he cupped my

cheek. I could feel the tremble in his fingers, but my brave fucking lion held my gaze and continued. "You know we've spoken about how I've never really wanted to kiss anyone before, except maybe the girl at school I told you about. But I like kissing you, and what we were doing just now..." His voice trailed off, and this time, he dropped his gaze.

I brought my hand up to curl around his, the one that was still cupping my cheek, still trembling against my skin. "What we were doing just now...?"

"I liked that, too. A lot. And I didn't want to stop. I've never...I've, um, obviously touched myself, but it's never felt like *that*."

"So." I exhaled shakily. "Wanna carry on?"

"Yes, if you want to," he whispered, hesitating for a second until I nodded, and then he pulled me down to him.

"Tell me if you want to stop anytime, and we can," I murmured against his lips, and his hum of agreement was swallowed by my mouth. I kissed him slow and deep, losing myself in the slide of his mouth against mine. What exactly was going to happen next, I had no clue. I was completely out of my depth here, but as usual, being like this with Leo felt...right. Despite the fact I was theoretically straight. Probably. Maybe. It was something I could think about later or never. Who cared right now when what we were doing felt this good?

My hands went to his hips, and I pulled him on top of me. He gasped, and then suddenly, the kiss wasn't slow and deep and soft. It was hard, and messy, and really fucking hot, with Leo rolling his hips down in a way that made my dick throb. Leo was just as hard against me, panting against my mouth as I dared to slide my hands lower onto the curve of his ass.

He ground down harder, a breathy moan falling from

his lips, and bloody hell, I was gonna make a serious mess of my joggers because it was so. Fucking. Hot. I palmed his firm ass, breaking our kiss so I could get at his jaw, dragging my teeth over the smooth skin.

"Finn. I think—I think I—I'm close. Can you touch me? Please?" His voice was wrecked, and the small "please" at the end did me in. As if I could ever refuse him anything. I rolled us to the side, getting my hand down inside his tented joggers, and then I was touching another man's dick for the first time in my life.

A dick that belonged to Leo.

Leo, who had his head thrown back, his eyes closed, and moans and pants falling from his mouth. Leo. Who wanted me to touch him. To be the first person to get to do this to him.

Fuck.

I stroked my hand down his length, hot and hard in my grip. When I stroked back up, I ran my thumb over the tip of his erection, smooth where his foreskin had retracted to expose the sensitive head, wet with precum. He gasped, then shuddered, and then his cock pulsed in my grip, stripes of cum shooting over my hand and the inside of his joggers. It was messy, and I was completely uncoordinated, but it was so fucking hot that all I needed to do was rub over my joggers with my free hand, and I was coming, too, my body curling forwards as my release hit me.

Our heavy breaths seemed abnormally loud in the ensuing silence. I wasn't sure what to do. My hand was kind of covered in Leo's cum—oh, and it was still inside his joggers, just casually resting against his spent cock. And there was the small matter of the uncomfortable wetness in my own joggers.

Totally worth it, though.

Leo broke the silence with a small huff of breathless laughter. "That was messier than I thought it would be."

"Yeah. We should plan it better next time." My eyes widened as I realised what I'd just implied. "Uh, if there's a next time."

I glanced over at him to find him smiling up at the ceiling, his eyes half-lidded and sleepy. "Oh, yeah. Next time."

Okay. Good. We could discuss that later. First, we needed to get cleaned up. Withdrawing my hand from Leo's joggers, accidentally smearing his release everywhere in the process, I grimaced.

"Shower? You can go first if you want. I'll get us some clean clothes."

He yawned as he nodded slowly. I had a sudden, overpowering urge to wrap him up and cuddle him until he fell asleep, which didn't even surprise me at this point. I'd just had my hand on his dick. Of course I was going to want to take care of him afterwards. But I resisted. First, shower and fresh clothes, then food, then sleep.

I froze in place as it hit me all over again. Fucking hell. I'd had my hand on Leo's dick.

Okay. I could panic about that later. I had more important priorities for now.

After we'd showered and changed and the food was on its way, both of us were feeling more awake, sprawled out over my bed and scrolling through Netflix as we tried to agree on something to watch while we ate. I grabbed our phones, handing Leo his and switching mine on. We'd both turned them off this morning, not wanting the real world to invade our planned gaming day.

As soon as my phone loaded up, it began buzzing, and next to me, Leo's was doing the same. I thumbed through my apps, reading the messages I'd received.

CHARLIE:

Are you ok? What happened last night?

Before I forget. See if Leo wants to come to your match on Sunday. We need to boost the supporter numbers!

You don't have to tell me what happened last night but let me know if you're ok

BENNETT:

LOOK WHAT LEO DID. THIS IS ALL HIS FAULT

There was a picture of Niccolò beaming and pointing at a TV screen, where Mario Kart was showing the podium awards. I laughed, thrusting my phone at Leo.

"Look. You're being blamed for this."

Leo grinned, shaking his head. "I only showed Nic what the buttons did and gave him a few tips. Maybe Bennett's not as good at the game as he thinks."

The fact he was happily joining in with the teasing, and teasing right back, made me warm all over.

ME:

Leo says you're just shit at Mario Kart

"Finn!" Leo screeched, trying to wrestle my phone out of my grip, but it was too late because I'd already hit Send. Laughing, I tussled with him for a couple of minutes until we somehow ended up with my hands buried in his soft hair, holding his face still while I kissed him.

With a groan, I pulled away, picking up my phone from where it had been discarded on the bed. I needed to stop getting carried away. Leo seemed to be of the same mind, straightening up and taking several deep breaths.

I tapped out another reply to Bennett, letting Leo see my screen.

ME:

> JK. He doesn't think that. I say you're shit though

Bennett replied with a middle finger emoji, and I grinned, sending him a kissing face before I returned to my message thread with Charlie.

ME:

> I'm good. All ok here, thanks for checking up on me. I'll ask Leo if he'll come to the match

"Leo?"

"Yeah?" He was staring down at his phone screen with that sweet, shy smile that was becoming one of my favourites.

"Do you wanna come to our match on Sunday? It's an away game. Charlie's asking."

He glanced over at me, his sweet smile disappearing. "Do...do you want me to come?"

"What? Of course I do!" Why would he ever think that I wouldn't want him there?

His lashes lowered. "Oh, okay. It's just...you didn't invite me, so I wasn't sure. I don't want to be a distraction or anything."

"Leo. No. You have an open invite to every single one of my future games, okay? And my practices. I would be over the fucking moon if you came. I just didn't want to put you in a situation where you felt like you had to say yes. I don't want you to be uncomfortable. The games are a lot more full-on than our training sessions." I shifted closer to him, placing my hand on his thigh. "I just want you to be happy."

His mouth fell open. "Oh."

"Why are you so surprised by this?" Without waiting for him to reply, because I knew this whole conversation was awkward for both of us, I continued talking. "Speaking of surprised, who texted you? I'm sure your phone vibrated more times than mine."

"JJ, and...Nic?" His voice lifted in a question, and my brows rose. Wordlessly, he handed me his phone, open to his messages.

JJ:

Hope you're ok babe. If Finn isn't looking after you say the word and I'll come straight over

You know I'll come over anytime. Here for you

You're strong and I know you can handle anything

I saw that he'd replied to JJ, telling him he was fine and not to worry. Beneath JJ's messages, there was a thread from an unknown number.

UNKNOWN:

Hope you don't mind I got your number from JJ

Are you ok? I'm good at keeping secrets if you want to talk

Especially sex related things

Did I say I have a FanBoyzOnly account?

> The only reason I mentioned that was because it means I'm confident discussing things

> I'm not bragging

I couldn't help laughing at what were clearly Niccolò's messages.

> UNKNOWN:
>
> Bennett said I should unsend these messages but I don't know how

> Sorry. All I wanted to say was that I hope you're ok and you can talk to me anytime because we're friends

There was a short break in the message time stamps, followed by a couple more.

> UNKNOWN:
>
> It's Nic BTW in case you didn't work it out!
> I owe you!

> Look at this!

Those messages were followed by the same picture Bennett had sent me.

"Nic," I said, and Leo nodded, that cute little smile appearing on his face again as he took his phone back and replied after adding Nic to his contacts. I looked away, not wanting to invade his privacy.

My phone beeped, letting me know our delivery was due to arrive, and so I jogged downstairs, throwing open the front door and surprising the girl standing on the driveway with her hand raised to the doorbell.

I relieved her of the bags of food, setting everything up on the kitchen table since I didn't have the space in my bedroom. When I called Leo and he came downstairs, I watched him carefully as he opened the individual cardboard boxes, waiting for the moment he realised—

"Finn!"

"Yeah?" Leaning back against the counter, I raised a brow.

"You got pizza?" He stared down into the open box, his eyes wide and so fucking green.

"Yeah. I knew you wanted it, so I ordered from the place that does pizza and chicken. See, I can compromise—"

He launched himself at me, and I automatically wrapped my arms around him, holding him in place.

"Best, best friend," he mumbled into my throat, and I grinned. When he lifted his head, I pressed a quick kiss to his nose, right over his smattering of freckles, and then handed him a plate.

"Help yourself before it gets cold."

With a bright smile, he did.

NINETEEN

LEO

"This is...busy." I eyed the crowds, automatically hunching in on myself, making myself smaller.

"Babe." Niccolò tucked his arm through mine, giving me a bright smile. "It's gonna be okay. Anyway, we need you here today. You're our resident football expert."

"I'm not an expert. I watch it on TV sometimes...and live, now, I guess," I mused as I kept my gaze fixed on Noah's back, following him and Elliot through the tiered stands to our seats. Charlie had been the one to invite me—via Finn—but he hadn't been able to make it in the end. I was saved from the stress of potentially letting Finn down rather than showing up alone when Niccolò had texted me to check if I was coming. Maybe "check" wasn't the right word since he'd basically told me I was coming with him. He'd taken charge, sorting everything out, and all I'd had to do was wait outside my block of flats this morning at the specified time.

Now, here we were.

"You and Elliot are the ones who know about football,"

Niccolò proclaimed. "You're way more of an expert than me and Noah."

"No, I don't think I am."

"You are." He gently tugged on my arm, and I realised we'd come to a stop. As we settled onto the hard plastic seats, Nic gave me another bright smile, and I realised at once what he'd been trying to do. Distract me, and he'd managed it successfully, too.

Thanks, I mouthed, and he nodded, bouncing in his seat happily.

"Hey, Leo."

I spun to face Noah. "Y-yeah?"

"Are you coming back to ours afterwards? *Mario Kart* rematch?"

"Me?" I stared at him. Why would he want me there? We didn't even know each other, and there was nothing interesting about me.

"Yeah. You're the only one who can give me a run for my money. I don't feel challenged playing any of the others." He smirked, and I couldn't help laughing. "Finn will want you there, anyway. If you're not there, he'll be texting you or talking about you, so you should just come and put him out of his misery."

My face warmed, and I shifted in my seat. "Um..."

"How is this my life?" Noah shook his head, changing the subject as if he realised I was uncomfortable. "Living with footballers, a footballer boyfriend, planning events for footballers and their—" At my sudden intake of breath, he paused. "Uh, their friends and whatever."

"You brought it on yourself when you started dating Liam," Elliot said from his other side.

"Yeah. I guess he's worth it, though." Noah sighed dramatically, then grinned. "It just hits me sometimes that this would have been my worst nightmare come true last year. It's weird how things work out."

In my head, I could hear Finn saying, *What about a dare? I dare you to speak to one person*, like he had when we'd been in the student union together and he'd been trying to give me flirting pointers. "O-oh? Why was it a nightmare?" I could do this. I could make conversation with someone.

"It's a long story, but I'll give you the highlights. When I was at school, there were some asshole footballers who made my life a misery..."

As he spoke, I found myself responding automatically, interjecting with comments and questions like we were having an actual conversation. We *were* having an actual conversation. And this confident guy had been through some of the same stuff I'd been through, too. Not bullied or teased for his shyness but singled out for being different. Somehow, knowing that gave me the confidence to speak to him like I would with my other friends.

My mind flashed back to my school days. Days I didn't like to think about. If I was completely honest with myself, though, I had changed. I'd come a long way since then, and I was doing better now, even if it didn't feel like it a lot of the time.

Our conversation came to a natural end when the teams came out, Nic pulling me to my feet with a strength that belied his size, clapping and cheering for the LSU team. The players knew the section we were seated in, and when my gaze found Finn's, he was already looking at me. When our eyes met, he gave me a huge, beaming smile, and I smiled back, suddenly shy. Okay, I was always shy, but the way he was looking at me, like he was just so happy to see me there...

Fuck. I should've come to one of his matches before this, shouldn't I? Even if it scared me. That was what best friends did. They supported each other. From now on, I was going to make it a priority to come to as many of his games as I could. Maybe I should bring Ed with me, too. I knew he'd been wanting to come and watch Finn play.

The game itself passed quickly, with Elliot and Noah disappearing at half-time and coming back with drinks and snacks for all of us. I bit down on my wobbly lip as I accepted their offerings, unable to believe that this was really happening to me and not wanting them to see how affected I was by their kind gestures. Niccolò leaned into me, placing his head on my shoulder, the way I'd seen him do with JJ, and squeezed my arm.

"They see you as one of us. You're our friend," he whispered, and my breath got caught in my throat.

"H-how did you know?" I managed. He gave me a sad smile.

"Babe, I can read you." My eyes widened, and he immediately shook his head, his face more serious than I'd ever seen it. "Not...it's not that obvious. I mean, it is to me. But I was there at the student union and at JJ's afterwards, wasn't I? And JJ's spoken about you to me. Not, like, gossiping or anything, just a few things he's mentioned that add up. People *like* you, you know. You're nice, and sweet, and Finn's a good guy, even though he ruined JJ's favourite shoes. He wouldn't be hanging out with you all the time if you were someone bad. No one cares if you're shy." He sucked in a breath. "No, they do care, but only about making you more comfortable. Do you understand?"

I couldn't speak. I swallowed around the lump in my throat. Distantly, I was aware of a whistle blowing and the second half of the game beginning, but I couldn't focus on anything except the words Niccolò had just spoken to me.

"Over here." Nic pulled me along, his glittery football hoodie sparkling in the sun, which had finally made an appearance. Most of the spectators had left, with just the friends and family of the teams milling around, waiting for the players to appear from the changing rooms. Nic came to a stop right in front of the doors because, unlike me, he loved being front and centre of everything. I did my best to block everything else out, and when Noah and Elliot joined us, chatting easily about the match, I found myself relaxing.

"Ben!" Niccolò screeched, tearing away from us as the doors opened, throwing himself at his boyfriend and kissing all over his face. Bennett staggered backwards, laughing as he dropped his bag and swept Nic up into his arms. Noah and Liam moved to greet their own boyfriends, and I was left alone for a second until Finn appeared from behind the others.

He walked over to me, coming to a stop in front of me and lowering his duffel bag to the floor, his gaze searching.

"Hi. How did you get on with the others?"

"Good." I moved closer. "Good."

"Good," he repeated, a smile curving over his lips.

"You were good. Really good." It was true. He'd worked so hard out on the pitch and been so focused, and I was so proud of him.

His smile widened. "Yeah? That's good."

I nodded, and he stepped even closer.

"Enough of the word 'good.' What's the protocol here? Am I allowed to hug my best friend?"

I didn't reply verbally. Instead, I closed the final bit of distance between us, wrapping my arms around his neck. He sighed against me, bringing his arms around my waist.

"Mmm, that's better. All my friends were getting hugs, and no one was hugging me."

I drew back, smiling at his fake pout. Sliding my hand around to the front of his neck, I brushed my thumb over his lip. "Poor baby."

"Aww. You called me baby, baby."

"Shut up," I mumbled. "I was calling you a baby. You said you didn't like nicknames."

"Maybe I might, if they come from you. Say it again."

"No."

"Yes." He was grinning so happily it made my stomach do a swooping thing. I liked it. A lot.

"Finn."

"Please, baby."

"Fuck off." I buried my head in the crook of his neck. "Baby."

"Ha! I knew I could get you to say it." His grip tightened, and with no warning, he spun us around, nearly sending us both to the floor as my leg tangled with his and I lost my balance. We righted ourselves, Finn shooting me a sheepish smile that gave me that same swooping feeling.

A throat cleared loudly from behind me. "As funny as it is to watch Finn almost face-plant the floor, we're waiting to go. I won't complain if you want to recreate it later, though. I'll video it."

When I turned, I saw Ander eyeing us with amusement, his hand clasped in Elliot's. He jerked his head towards the car park. "Come on. We're in the minibus. Leo, Noah's driving you and E back with Nic."

"Oh, yeah. Thanks." I'd forgotten all about everything

else around me, but now, everything filtered back in—the warm sun, the distant murmur of voices, and the noise of car engines starting up. Finn scooped up his bag, and we followed Ander and Elliot over to the car park, Finn's arm brushing against mine. When we reached Noah's car, Finn stopped, leaning in and pressing his mouth to my ear.

"So fucking proud of you," he whispered. I felt his lips brush over my earlobe in a soft kiss, and then he was stepping backwards, lifting his hand in a wave. "See you at Ander's house."

When I climbed into the back seat of Noah's VW Golf, Noah, Elliot, and Niccolò were deep in a heated discussion about the music that should be played on the drive back to campus, and I relaxed back against the headrest. No one was looking at me, or had been spying on me with Finn, or anything else my paranoid brain could conjure up.

I smiled.

———

"I didn't come last!" Niccolò bounced in Bennett's lap, waving his controller in the air. "Thanks, Leo."

"Oh. No. It's all you. I didn't do anything."

Finn leaned down, wrapping his arms around my shoulders. "Accept the thanks."

I tilted my head so I could see him. He was seated on one of the sofas while I was sprawled on the floor in front of him, using a cushion propped up against his legs as a backrest. "Okay," I said. I got a kiss to the cheek for that, and I couldn't help my gaze darting around the room to see if anyone noticed. There were fewer people here than there had been at the football night, but there were still plenty of witnesses.

No one was looking, though, other than Noah, who simply raised a brow, tapping his controller. I nodded, and he elbowed Liam, getting him to pass his controller to me. We were playing casually—no tournament this time—but Noah had specifically asked me for a rematch, and now I had something to prove.

"A kiss for luck," Finn murmured, brushing his lips over my cheek again before he released me, straightening up. My stomach was doing that swooping thing again, but I didn't have time to think about what it meant right now. My reputation was at stake here.

We lined up—me, Noah, Preston, and their housemate Damon, and then the countdown began. Adrenaline flooded my body as I gripped the controller with sweaty palms.

Go.

We shot away from the start line.

"Fuck, yes, baby." Finn had leaned forwards again, and now he was speaking low in my ear. "You're ahead. Come on. You can do it." I let his words filter through my brain as I skidded around the final bend, swerving to avoid a banana, the finish line in my sights. Noah was right on my heels—or wheels, I guessed—and I couldn't afford to let him get past me. Except he tapped his controller lightly, knocking me to the left, and I lost precious seconds correcting my steering. We crossed the finish line at almost exactly the same time, but the display told me that Noah had won again, just milliseconds ahead of me.

"Good game." Noah turned to me with a bright grin. "You almost had me until I knocked you off course."

"That was a dirty trick. I wish I'd thought of it first."

"Next time."

We smiled at each other, and behind me, Finn squeezed

my shoulders before circling his thumbs over my nape. His head was still lowered, dipping to my ear. "You almost had him."

"Movie time!" Ander announced. "Travis is dicking down his girlfriend, so that means I get to choose what we watch."

Liam threw a cushion at him. "Why do you get to choose? You don't even live here."

"Guest privileges. Tell him, Noah."

Noah held up his hands. "Don't get me involved in this."

"Wanna go?" Finn murmured quietly. "We haven't been to your flat for a while."

I was taken aback by the rush of blood from my head to a certain other part of my body. He probably meant he wanted to play games, but I hoped he wanted to kiss me. Or maybe even more. Fuck, I wanted that.

I nodded, and he helped me to my feet, mumbling an excuse about coursework that no one bought, going by the smirks and knowing expressions. Somehow, I was okay with the teasing, mainly because my dick was doing the thinking for me. That was a novel experience.

As soon as we got back to my bedroom, Finn dropped his bag to the floor and then sat down in my gaming chair. He placed a set of headphones over his ears, handing me my own headphones, and wiggled the mouse to wake up the computer. I did my best to ignore the sudden disappointment heavy in my stomach. My monitor was still on the *Lesath Legends* home screen because we'd played a marathon online session against each other last night after I'd eventually left Finn's house, and when Finn picked up the controller he normally used when he was here, I forced a smile. Okay, we were playing. This was good. I liked playing my favourite game with my favourite person. The other stuff wasn't important.

"Leo."

"What."

"Come here." Finn patted his lap, and I sat sideways on him. I could feel his gaze boring into the side of my head.

"Now what? Are we playing?"

He hummed. "Not yet. First of all, I have a dare for you."

I couldn't help stiffening. "What is it?"

Taking the headphones from my grip, he carefully placed them over my ears. The sound was a little muffled with them on, but I could still hear him easily.

"You look cute with those on. I dare you to tell me what you thought was going to happen when we came back here."

"Th-that's not a dare! It's a truth."

"Leo."

When I looked at him, he was smiling, but he seemed a little unsure and a little hopeful. I inhaled, then exhaled.

"I didn't think...it wasn't what I thought was going to happen. I guess I wanted to...you know. Kiss or something. But only if you wanted to. I'm happy to play."

The uncertainty disappeared from his expression, and I returned his smile. Wrapping his arms around me, he leaned in. "I set this up because I didn't wanna pressure you into doing anything. I thought if I did it straight away, you wouldn't have to be worrying about whether I wanted to kiss you, or—" He broke off with a shake of his head. "I dunno. I just didn't want you to be uncomfortable or feel pressured."

My arms went around his neck of their own accord. "I'm not." Turning away, I glanced at my bed. "We...we might be more comfortable over there. I'm not sure if Secretlab made their gaming chairs with, uh, that in mind."

"That?" He leaned in, smiling against the side of my face. "By 'that,' I hope you mean kissing."

"And maybe more," I said breathlessly.

"Fuck." He groaned. "Yeah. Yes. More. Okay. Bed."

Both of us ended up laughing as we ripped off our headphones and Finn threw the controller onto my desk, almost upending the chair as we scrambled to get to the bed. My humour died away when Finn had me on my back, pressing soft kisses across my face, and then took my lower lip between his teeth, biting down so gently that a whole flurry of butterflies erupted in my stomach.

Oh. That was what that swooping feeling had been earlier.

"Finn."

"Yeah, baby?" He nipped at my jaw.

"Can I touch you today?" It was all I'd been able to think about since he'd made me come with his hand. It had felt so good, and while I was under no illusions that I'd be any good at it, I wanted to try.

A huff of breath skated across my skin as he lowered his head, burying it in my throat. "Fucking hell, Leo. Yeah. Course. You can do anything you want to me."

"Anything?"

"Anything."

TWENTY

FINN

When I raised my head, Leo was staring at me, all huge green eyes and soft, parted lips. He looked more kissable than anyone I'd seen, ever. I didn't know what that said about me except that I was way out of my depth, and literally the only thing my brain and dick could agree on was that letting him touch me was a very, very good idea.

I kissed him again, because I could, and it was clear that he wanted me to. It was such an addictive feeling, getting lost in his mouth, his body against mine. So familiar by now but still so new because we'd both reached the point where we were turned on by what we were doing and wanted to take things further.

When we broke apart, I trailed kisses across his jaw and up to his ear.

"Remember, if you want to stop, just say the word, and we can stop, no questions asked."

He ran his hand down my back. "That goes for you, too."

"Yeah." I kissed him again, right below his earlobe, making him shiver. His hard cock was digging into my thigh, and fuck me, it was making my own cock even harder.

"Can we—"

My head rose, finding him biting down on his lip, his lashes downcast.

"Hey. Tell me." I brought my hand up to his face, gently tugging his lip out from between his teeth. "You know you can tell me anything."

He swallowed, his Adam's apple bobbing, and I ducked down to kiss it.

"Can we maybe...get naked?"

Fuuuuck. I hadn't expected him to go there, not yet, but now the question was out there, whispered against me like a secret, and honestly, I was as nervous as he was. This was taking our friendship to a whole new level.

"Uh. Shit. Sorry. Never mind. Can we pretend I didn't say anything?"

It took me a second to realise that Leo had stiffened beneath me, his words coming out in a panicked rush. Oh, fuck. I'd been so lost in my head that I hadn't even responded to his question.

"Yes. No. I mean, fuck. Sorry." Pressing my face into the pillow next to him, I groaned. *Okay, try again, Finn.* Lifting my head, I stroked my fingers through his hair, brushing it away from his eyes as I met his gaze. "Leo. Sorry. I was thinking...complete honesty here, I'm nervous."

"You are?"

"Yeah."

His brows pulled together. "Why?"

"Uh...because I don't really know what I'm doing here... what *we're* doing here. I've also never been naked with another man before, not counting communal changing rooms. I don't want to do anything wrong."

His lips curved into an O, and his eyes widened, dark pupils eclipsing the green. He looked so fucking gorgeous, all turned on and wanting me. I couldn't even believe this was happening.

He blinked and shook his head, dislodging my hand that was resting in his hair. "I didn't even think about that. I thought you knew what you were doing."

"I really, really don't."

"Oh. Okay. Maybe...maybe we can work it out together?"

"Yeah?" My lips curved upwards.

"Yeah."

Where to start? Kissing. Kissing was good and safe, and we knew what we were doing there. We were pretty much experts by this point. Just as I lowered my head, Leo's hand slid down my back to the hem of my T-shirt, and he slipped his fingers beneath, onto the bare skin of my back. I could feel them tremble against me, but he stroked upwards. How could one simple touch feel so good?

"Off," he murmured, and if that was what he wanted, that was what I was going to give him. I lifted myself upright, moving to straddle his thighs, and then I tugged my T-shirt off. His gaze darkened as he dragged it down my body, stopping when it reached the obvious tent in my shorts. Then he licked his lips, and that was fucking *it*.

"Off, now," I said hoarsely, pushing his T-shirt up. I needed to feel his skin against mine right now. My little lion arched upwards, the graceful movement of his body a complete contrast to the way he yanked his T-shirt off impatiently, throwing it somewhere on the floor. The next thing I knew, I was lying on top of him, all that warm, bare skin beneath me, and he was grasping at my shoulders, pulling me closer. As if we could even get any closer. Our kisses became deeper as we rolled around on the bed, hands touching every inch of bare skin. My dick was harder than it had ever been, and I was almost certain that Leo was in the same predicament as I was.

"Baby," I panted, rubbing my fingers over the waistband of his shorts. "Wanna take these off?"

"Mmm. Please." He was so fucking hot, writhing beneath me, and I couldn't get enough. He ducked his head. "Same time?"

I melted for him.

"Anything you want. Anything." I rolled off him, my hand going to my shorts. "Now?"

His response was a jerky nod, and in the space of fifteen seconds, we were both fully naked in front of each other for the first time. Leo curled over, and doing my best to ignore my own nerves, because I was naked in front of him for the first time, I reached out, stroking down his arm.

"Let me see you, baby. Please."

He flushed, his eyes squeezing shut, but he slowly uncurled his body, baring himself to my gaze. He was so fucking brave, and he was giving me his trust, and it was a fucking gift.

I was saying the words before I could think them through, not even caring how inappropriate they probably were for me to say to a friend. He needed to know.

"You're so fucking beautiful, Leo."

His eyes flew open. "Really?"

The sheer disbelief in his voice had my throat threatening to close up. How did he not know how gorgeous he was?

"Really, Leo. I'd never lie to you." Shifting closer, I placed my finger on his forehead. I'd already said the words, so I might as well commit. He needed to know I was telling the truth. "You're beautiful from your head." I trailed my finger downwards, over his nose, onto his lips, where I pressed down lightly. His mouth curved upwards. Shifting farther down the bed, I kept going, over his throat, and onto his torso, all the way to his belly button. I paused, glancing back up at him. He was watching my finger, fascinated, and I smiled. Bypassing his erect cock for now, I continued down his thigh, then onto his leg, finally finishing at his feet. I tapped his big toe.

"To your toes," I said.

"Finn." His smile was so wide.

"It's true. Do you believe me now?"

"No, but I'm working on it."

"Good. Keep working on it." Crawling back up the bed, I kissed his smiling mouth. "Ready for more?" My heart was pounding, but I refused to let my nerves overtake me.

In reply, he wrapped his arms around me, pulling me on top of him again, and oh. Topless Leo had been a turn-on, but a completely naked Leo, hard and willing, with the wet tip of his cock rubbing against my skin, was another level.

"Finn." The way he breathed my name was so fucking addictive. "What do we do now?"

I wanted his hands on me. Badly.

"You said you wanted to touch me earlier. Do you still—"

"Yes. That. Please."

"Okay." I pressed a kiss to his lips, which turned into his tongue sliding against mine, both of us so hard and gasping for breath when we separated. With an effort, I rolled onto my side, gripping his hand and ignoring the shake in both of our fingers as I threaded mine between his.

"I—" he began before cutting himself off, swallowing hard. A determined expression overtook his face. "No. I want this. Just...tell me if I'm doing it wrong." With those words, he tugged his hand out of mine and placed his palm flat on my chest, carefully sliding it down my torso. When he reached my lower stomach, he glanced back up at me, and then he lifted his hand, carefully wrapping his fingers around the base of my cock. He let out a small gasp that made me smile and turned me on all at the same time—how the fuck did he always manage to do that to me?—then experimentally stroked his hand upwards.

"So good. A bit tighter. Yeah, that's it." I continued to encourage him while trying not to lose my mind over the way he was making me feel. His movements grew more confident, more forceful, just the way I liked it. I groaned, thrusting into his grip, and reached out, getting my hand around his dick. It was easier this time because there were no clothes in the way, and I could properly appreciate the sight of him, naked and flushed and panting, with my hand fisting his cock.

It was like a chain reaction, giving and receiving, and Leo came just seconds before me, my hand covering his when his grip on me loosened. Struggling to regain my breath, I flopped onto my back, glancing down at the mess covering me. Ah, well. Totally worth it.

I twisted my head to press a kiss to Leo's cheek. "That was so good."

His lips curved upwards. "I'm glad I got to do that with you."

I returned his smile. "Me too."

TWENTY-ONE

LEO

R ubbing my temples, I did my best to ignore my phone as it lit up again. Another message. I knew I needed to reply, but I also needed to get rid of this headache, not to mention the nausea that wouldn't go away. Everything had seemed so simple, and then it wasn't.

I'd given Finn Carsley a hand job. I'd actually done it, and he'd reciprocated. I didn't regret any of it, far from it. What was making my head spin was the fact that Finn had seemed to take it all in his stride, like it was nothing out of the ordinary. I was driving myself mad wondering if he'd really liked what we'd done, if he was just being polite when he said he had, whether he really had liked my body or had just been caught up in the moment...

My overthinking brain was already struggling with all that from the minute I woke up, but then I'd received an email from my computing lecturer. The nausea was already churning in my stomach from the minute I read the subject line—"important project presentation details"—and only intensified when I read the email itself.

I was expected to do a presentation as part of my group

project. I'd already known—and avoided thinking about—that fact, but what I hadn't known was that I had to do part of it completely on my own. Our group had all been given a different area of the project to focus on for our presentation, based on our strongest skill sets. The presentation would begin with all project partners showcasing our booking website, and then Connor and Niall would take their turns to present their own individual sections. Their individual presentations would be followed by mine. Alone. Worst of all, I had to do it in front of industry professionals.

My feelings were so overwhelming I was struggling to breathe. Feelings of inadequacy, fear of being laughed at, of making a fool of myself, of people judging me behind my back and to my face...it was too much.

I'd thought I'd struggled before my dance showcase, but this was something far, far worse. At least with my dance showcase, when Finn had dared me to do it, I could fool myself into pretending that no one was watching me. The audience was in darkness, silent as they took in the routine, listening to the accompanying music. There would be no way to trick my brain with this. Nowhere to hide. No Finn supporting me in the audience. No Connor and Niall at my side to help me through when I stumbled over my words and my mind went blank.

"Leo?" Connor's voice came through the door, followed by a knock, and I quickly rubbed my hand across my face, hoping the outside of me was less of a mess than the inside.

"Come in," I croaked, and the door opened, Connor entering my bedroom, followed by Niall.

"You got the email, too," Niall said, glancing at my monitor, which still displayed the message from my lecturer. "Can't believe they're making us do part of it on our own. How are you feeling, man? Remember what happened last time we did a presentation?"

My stomach sank. Just when I thought I couldn't feel any worse about it.

"Niall!" Connor smacked his arm, and he grimaced.

"Sorry. Yeah. Nah, it'll be fine. We'll make sure you're ready, don't worry. We've got your back."

I appreciated their support, but it didn't stop the feeling of sheer dread that filled me. "I just hope I don't fuck it up. I can't... I didn't know we'd have to do it on our own. In front of industry professionals."

"Yeah. The worst part is gonna be the questions."

Questions? I frantically scanned the email, my hand clamping over my mouth when I got to the part of the message I hadn't read yet because I'd been too busy panicking about having to do a presentation in the first place.

Up to ten minutes allowed for questions from the panel.

The panel, which consisted of my lecturer, another member of the computing faculty, and two industry professionals.

"I feel sick," I mumbled, doubling over and trying to remember how to breathe.

"It's gonna be okay. You did good in our last presentation after you remembered what to say." Niall tried to reassure me, but his words seemed meaningless. One, because we all knew how much I'd struggled to do it, and two, because my brain would never convince me otherwise.

"Why is my brain like this?" I lowered my head to my desk, closing my eyes.

Connor cleared his throat. "Give me your hand." I obediently held out my hand, and he pressed something cool and hard onto the pad of my index finger. He muttered something to himself that I didn't catch, and then he spoke more loudly. "Finn...? No, it's Connor... Yeah, he's, uh, I guess he's okay, but I think you should come over... Yeah, right now, if you're free... Alright, see you soon."

I lifted my head from the desk, staring at him. "Did you just call Finn from my phone?"

He nodded. "Thank me later. Wanna play a bit of FIFA while we're waiting?" Before I could reply either way, he forcibly dragged me out of my chair and down the hallway to our tiny communal area. He pushed me down on the sofa, handed me a controller, and he and Niall took a seat on either side of me, trapping me in place.

Their distraction technique worked for a little while, getting me out of my head as I focused on the game, but then the guilt began to pile up. People always had to go out of their way for me. No one else seemed to be this fucking needy. My friends were having to sit here and stop me from spiralling into a panic attack instead of whatever else they'd been planning to do, and now Finn was having to come here when I knew for a fact he had a study session planned today with some of his course mates.

Why can't you be normal? I asked myself for the thousandth time.

"Sorry," I muttered.

Next to me, Connor sighed. "Don't."

"But—"

"The S-word is banned. C'mon, don't worry about anything else. Just play."

"Yeah. We're about to win this match," Niall added, knocking me with his shoulder, and I breathed out. Okay. My brain was twisting my thoughts again. Fucking hell, being in my head was exhausting.

The doorbell sounded, and Connor paused the game,

jumping up. When he returned, he had Finn in tow. Finn, who looked a little out of breath, like he'd been running—

Everything crashed down on me at once. I turned on him, my words lashing through the space between us. "Did you run here?"

His eyes widened. "Uh. I needed the exercise?" He gave me a sheepish smile.

"Yeah, the fit footballer needs exercise." I launched myself to my feet. "Stop, all of you! I don't want to be this huge fucking burden where you feel like you have to come running every time you think I might start spiralling. It makes me feel even worse, and you're having to go out of your way to fucking babysit me when you've got much better things to do with your time. I don't need you to do this, okay? I don't want you to! I'm fine on my own! Just fucking stop!"

There was a stunned silence, and I gasped, clapping my hand over my mouth, horrified at my outburst.

But there was no taking the words back.

"Shit. I-I'm sorry," I whispered and fled the room, barricading myself in my bedroom with a locked door and a chair in front of it for good measure.

My actions were predictably followed by a hammering on the wood, making the door vibrate.

"Leo!"

Connor.

I ignored him, and the banging eventually stopped. Collapsing onto my bed with stinging eyes, I stared up at the ceiling. I'd just managed to mess things up with three of my friends in one go, and I wasn't sure if they'd even forgive me. They *shouldn't* forgive me.

I didn't know how much time had passed, but eventually, I crawled from my bed, feeling like crying all over again when I curled up in the gaming chair Finn had bought me. I jammed my headphones over my stupid overgrown hair and loaded *Lesath Legends*. It was my one guaranteed escape from the world, and I needed it right now.

The in-game message alert was blinking at me. I thought about ignoring it, but I knew I wouldn't be able to focus on the game while I was wondering what was waiting for me. Steeling myself, I clicked on the message.

HAMMERHEAD:

I unlocked the abyss campaign. Want to play?

Oh, Finn. Hammerhead's icon showed he was online, and so I replied. There was only one answer I could give him because I didn't want to hurt him any more than I already had.

VIKING:

Ok

HAMMERHEAD:

We got this Viking. Ready up

VIKING:

Ready

Even though my headset was on mute, I could feel Finn there through the screen. He was too good to me, and I didn't deserve his understanding. Even after those things I'd said, he was still here, not making any demands of me, just letting me be and giving me what he somehow instinctively knew I needed.

We played for hours, communicating only through the in-game text chat, doing one campaign after the other. When the rumbling of my stomach became too loud to ignore, I typed out a single message with shaking hands, trying to brace myself for potential rejection.

VIKING:

Want to get some food?

He replied immediately.

HAMMERHEAD:

Yeah. Now?

VIKING:

Yes. I can come to you

HAMMERHEAD:

Unlock your door

His icon instantly greyed out, showing he was offline, and so I logged out, removing my headphones, and unlocked my door.

When I opened it, I stopped dead.

Finn was standing outside.

We stared at one another for a moment, both frozen in place, and then he sighed.

"Come here." He held out his arms, and when I remained where I was, he stepped forwards, wrapping his arms around me. I buried my face in the crook of his neck, breathing in the spiced apple scent of his shampoo. Stroking up and down my back, he remained silent, allowing me time to process what was happening.

"H-how are you here?" I mumbled into his throat.

"I never left. I persuaded Connor to let me use his laptop to play."

"I...I'm sorry. So sorry. I didn't mean what I said. Or...I guess I meant it, but I didn't mean to shout at you all."

"Leo." His voice was so sad. "I wish you could see yourself the way we see you. You're never a burden. I'm gonna tell you that as many times as it takes to sink in, even if it means I'm still telling you when we're in our eighties."

"Y-you still want to be my friend?"

"You did not just ask me that." Fuck, now he was pissed off.

"Sorry," I whispered.

"Okay. No." He drew back, releasing me for a second before he clasped my jaw, forcing me to meet his gaze. "You. Are. My. Family. That means we stick together. End of fucking discussion."

I licked my dry lips, keeping my eyes on his despite my instinct to turn away, to protect myself. "You're mine."

At my words, something hot flashed in his gaze. "I'm yours?"

"M-my family."

"I'm yours, and you're mine." There was something in his expression that I couldn't read, but it gave me chills. It was selfish of me because we still hadn't sorted anything out, but I wanted more of it.

Bringing my hand up, I mirrored his grip on my face, curling my fingers around his jaw. His stubble was sandpapery beneath the pads of my fingers where he hadn't bothered to shave. My finger brushed over his pulse point, and I could feel it beating wildly against my skin.

"I'm yours," I repeated, watching his eyes darken.

"Yes, you are, and don't you fucking forget it," he ground out, wrapping his hand around the back of my neck and yanking me into him. His lips came down on mine as I reached for him, both of us on exactly the same page.

"Finn," I gasped out, pulling him back into my bedroom, kicking the door shut behind us. "Finn."

"I've got you."

Fuck, this was nothing like the last time we'd done anything together. There was no hesitance as we ripped off our clothes in between frantic, messy kisses, got onto the bed, and then Finn was tightly gripping a handful of my hair, tugging my head back to expose my throat, biting and sucking.

I rutted up, my dick so hard it hurt, gripping onto him, digging the pads of my fingers into the muscles of his back as he marked me up in a way I'd never even contemplated before.

"You like that?" He mouthed across my skin. "Every time you look in the mirror and see this, you'll remember not to question what you mean to me."

"Fuck. Finn. Let me, please." I had no idea what I was doing, but I wanted to mark him in the same way so he knew how important he was to me. How seriously I took him. This. Us. Our friendship. Rolling us to the side, I got my mouth on his throat, licking over the salt of his skin before sucking hard, imitating his movements. I kept up the pressure until I was sure it had worked, and then I drew back, smiling when I saw the mark blooming on his skin.

"Impressed with yourself?"

I blinked up at him. His eyes were so dark, and goosebumps erupted over my skin at the way he was looking at me. No one had ever looked at me the way he did.

Instead of replying to his question, I pushed down on his shoulder. "Move onto your back, and let me show you how sorry I am."

He shifted onto his back, bringing his hand up to push my hair back from my face. "I already told you, you don't need to apologise."

"I do." Before I could talk myself out of it, I moved down the bed, settling between his thighs, my head directly above his erection. Even though I was committed to this, I needed—no, I *wanted* that final push.

"Dare me," I said.

"Fucking hell," he groaned. "You're killing me here."

"Dare me."

"Fuck. I dare you to suck my cock."

Wrapping my fingers around the base of his erection, still just as fascinating to me as the first time I'd touched him, I lowered my head. I hadn't told Finn, but I'd done a bit of online research, and while the videos had done absolutely nothing for me—only Finn seemed to have this effect on my libido—I had a vague idea of what I was supposed to do.

I flattened my tongue and licked across the head of his dick. He groaned again, and the sound encouraged me to keep going. I licked again, tasting his precum on my tongue. I couldn't really describe the taste because it was like nothing I'd tasted before, and I wasn't sure if I even liked it yet, but what I did like was Finn's reaction. He quickly shoved some pillows behind him to prop himself up, and then he buried his hands in my hair, tracking my movements with his intense, darkened gaze and parted lips. He'd told me I was beautiful before, but the way *he* looked right now was incomparable. I shifted, pressing my hips down into the bed to get some friction on my dick as I licked all around the head of his cock, and then down his shaft.

"Fuck, baby. You're gonna make me come so hard," he panted, his thighs tensing as he held himself still while I dragged my tongue all over his cock, getting it wet and messy. When I took the tip into my mouth, his grip tightened in my hair, moans falling from his throat as I took more and more of him in, doing my best to breathe through my nose as my lips stretched around his girth.

"Leo," he choked out, tugging urgently at my hair, and I pulled back, but he was still in my mouth when he started to come, his cock pulsing as the first hit of his release went down my throat. Quickly closing my eyes, I pulled all the way back, feeling his cum landing on my face. I did my best to stroke him through it until his hand came down over mine, stilling my movements.

Collapsing down against his thigh, I pressed my cheek against his warm skin as I tried to catch my breath. I lazily rolled my hips down to keep up the much-needed friction on my dick, the sheets beneath me damp with my precum.

I'd just done that. I'd sucked Finn's dick, and he'd come from it. Why was that so hot? Fuck, I needed to come, too.

"Give me five seconds to recover, and I'll help you out with that."

"Hmm?"

"You said you needed to come, and I'll help you with that. Leo. You don't even know... That was fucking incredible," he breathed.

I'd said I needed to come out loud? I groaned, pressing my face into his leg, smearing his cum across his skin. Then, the rest of his words filtered through my brain. Incredible?

There was no time to think about it because Finn was already moving, and I found myself on my back with his head between my legs. I didn't let my nerves overtake me this time because the way he was looking at me left no room for doubts. He wanted me, and I wanted him in return.

"You look fucking hot with my cum on you," he murmured, scanning every inch of my face. "So fucking hot."

"Y-you look hot," I whispered, a confession he needed to hear as much as I needed to say it.

"*Baby.*" His tongue swiped across his lips, leaving them

glistening. Lowering his gaze to my erection, I saw him swallow hard. "I might not be any good at this."

His lips closed over the head of my dick, and he sucked lightly. I gasped, my hand flying to my mouth. This was a feeling so different from anything else I'd ever experienced. I hadn't even been able to imagine what it would feel like, and as his tongue carefully slid over my tip, I lost myself in the sensations coursing through me, ramping my entire body up so I was tingling all over, my dick aching and leaking, encompassed by the wet, hot suction of Finn's mouth.

"So good," I moaned, needing him to know how he was making me feel.

He hummed in acknowledgement, and, *oh.*

"Fuck. Do that again."

Another hum, and I gasped, my head falling back against the pillows. My entire body was on edge, poised, and with another swipe of his tongue, he tipped me over. Everything became a blur as my cock pulsed out ropes of cum, my mind going blissfully blank. When I came to, Finn was wiping at his face and coughing a little.

"I need to work on my swallowing technique," he said in between coughs, still somehow managing to grin at me. "Practice makes perfect."

He was perfect. So perfect.

"I need more practice, too." I returned his smile. "Finn, that was...that was—"

"Yeah?" His grin grew even wider, and I needed to keep telling him these things if it meant I got to see him looking like that.

"Yeah. The best."

"The only."

"Still the best."

He crawled up my body, flopping down next to me, and then pulled me into his arms for a wet and messy kiss.

"We need to clean up."

"We do. Why is sex so messy? Is it just us?" I wondered aloud, and he laughed, kissing the end of my nose.

"I like it messy with you. We have fun, don't we?"

"We do." I was the luckiest person in the whole world, and in that moment, I didn't want to change myself. I just wanted to be that person who made Finn as happy as he was right now. "I am sorry for earlier, though."

"I know, baby. I think your apology was more than sufficient." He leered at me, and we both dissolved into laughter. It wasn't even that funny, but I guess the endorphins were getting to us or something.

My stomach growled again, reminding me I'd invited him to get food with me before we'd been sidetracked by blow jobs.

"Food," I said. "Let's clean up, and I'll treat you to lunch."

Over plates of peri-peri chicken and chips, Finn and I discussed the idea that had been building in my mind on our walk to Nando's. I needed to be proactive. I was under no illusion that I was going to magically become a confident person, but what I could do was take steps to ensure I was as prepared as possible.

"You can do this. It's a solid plan, and you know I'll do everything I can to support you. You're not a burden, and it makes me happy to help you out whenever and wherever I can," Finn said.

He was so good to me. "Thank you. I...am going to try to believe that, I promise."

Squeezing my hand, he dunked a chip into his sauce. "Like I said, I'll keep telling you for as long as it takes to sink in."

I smiled. "I know we talked about me apologising earlier, but I also wanted to say sorry for taking you away from your study session."

He waved his chip in the air in a dismissive gesture, sauce flying off the end and splatting on the table. "Oops. Yeah, no, it's all good. Bennett's sending me the notes, and I'm ahead, anyway. I think I got quite a good deal out of it anyway, didn't I? A gaming session followed by an amazing BJ, and then my best friend treated me to my favourite chicken. What's not to love?"

I laughed, glad we were seated in a secluded booth so there was no one to overhear our conversation. "When you put it like that, I guess I did you a favour."

"Yeah, you did." His grin was huge. "Feel free to repeat it anytime."

"Without the part where I have a minor breakdown and shout at you all. Speaking of, I need to apologise to Connor and Niall and let them know about the plan." Pulling out my phone, I sent a message to our group chat.

ME:

> I'm really sorry for flying off the handle this morning. I didn't mean what I said and I appreciate you both looking out for me

> I've come up with a plan with Finn to help with the presentation but I'd like your input. If you're both around later we could go through it?

CONNOR:

No apologies necessary. Yeah I'll be back at the flat in about an hour for the rest of the day so I'm all yours

Not yours in that way if Finn reads this

ME:

He's my friend

NIALL:

What Con said. Also not yours in that way

Placing my phone down, I folded my arms on the tabletop and rested my head on them with a groan.

"What's wrong?"

"Look at the chat if you want. They're insinuating things again."

Finn chuckled under his breath as he read through the messages. "Fuck's sake." His hand stroked over my hair, and when I lifted my head from my arms, he shrugged, dipping another chip into his sauce. "Let them think what they want. We know the truth."

He was right. On that note, I tapped out a brief reply to let them know I'd be back in a couple of hours and then muted the chat.

It was time to finalise our plan. This presentation was going to be the best one we'd ever done. I'd make sure of it.

TWENTY-TWO

FINN

"What's this for?" Niall held up a rubber mallet.

I pointed towards the bag containing the tent pegs. "That's for the tent pegs in that bag."

"What are the pegs for?"

"To stop the tent collapsing." Connor cuffed him around the back of the head. "Isn't that obvious?"

"I told you I'm a city boy. I've never camped before. We'd better have the best presentation ever after all this shit. Tent pegs," he muttered, shaking his head.

Leaving Connor and Niall to figure out their own tent, I stepped over to where Leo was sprawled out on a blanket on the grass, his laptop open in front of him.

"Hi," he said, glancing up at me, shading his eyes. A bright smile curved over his lips. "I think I did it."

"Yeah?" I sank down next to him. "Show me."

We'd come to this little campsite on a farm in Surrey as a research trip so the boys could figure out the whole booking process from start to finish. They'd arranged to speak to the campsite owners and other campers about the kinds of things they looked for in a booking system, to ensure they were covering all their bases. Aiming for the highest possible grades, they were even designing a functioning site that would allow people to go through the entire booking process from beginning to end, choosing dates, pitch types, and optional extras.

The three of them had spent a long time talking—and Leo had apologised in person, not that he needed to, brainstorming ways they could support each other. It had taken Leo by surprise when his friends had shared that they were both nervous, and when it had sunk in, he'd stepped up his game.

What had started out as a vague idea to get Leo more comfortable with the upcoming presentation so he'd be able to answer any of the questions thrown at him had morphed into a comprehensive plan, a big part of which involved me ransacking my family's supply of camping equipment. Oh, and borrowing my dad's SUV for the night...which he'd finally agreed to after I promised I'd treat it with the utmost care.

Connor was the only other one who'd been camping before, although his version of camping had been at a festival with a pop-up tent he couldn't even remember sleeping in, so it made sense for them to come to an actual working campsite for research. And so here we were, on a sunny afternoon in a quiet field, and I got to spend a whole night with Leo, just the two of us in a tent.

"You really want to see?" Leo's brows pulled together, and I reached out, stroking my thumb over the furrow.

"Really. I might not understand it all, but it's important to you, and therefore, it's important to me."

"You know your stuff is important to me, too?" There was a question in his voice.

"Yeah. I know that. Anytime you wanna hear about engineering, I'm your man."

"I'll listen, even if I don't understand it. Like you do for me."

"That's because we're a team." I smiled at him, and he rose onto his elbows, pressing a quick kiss to my lips.

My stomach swooped.

"Oi, you two! Save it for your alone time in your tent! Leo, c'mon! We've got work to do."

Leo pulled away from me, all flushed cheeks and shy smiles, and how was he so fucking cute?

"Yeah, yeah." I gave Connor the finger, and he grinned at me. Leo clambered to his feet with a sigh, and then the three of them disappeared from the camping field to investigate the site facilities for their website. Because this was supposed to be a working trip, I made a half-hearted attempt to make some notes from the textbook I'd brought with me, but I gave up after a few minutes. I was ahead anyway, so it wasn't like I really *needed* to be working. Instead, I opened my phone to my internet browser.

Scrolling past my eighty-seven open tabs to the page I'd bookmarked, I began to read.

I didn't want this to be premeditated, and I didn't want to ever put any pressure on Leo, or on myself, but I wanted to make sure that if the topic of anal sex came up, we weren't going in blind. Although I'd slept with several girls in the past, this was a whole different ball game. Literally. It wasn't something I particularly wanted to ask anyone I knew for advice on, even though I had plenty of friends who I knew would be more than willing to share their experiences. This was private, between me and Leo, and the last thing we needed was even more questions about our friendship.

As I scrolled through the page, apprehension filled me. This was...daunting. Lube—yeah, I could do that, no problem. But the stretching thing with dildos or fingers or whatever...and who decided whose dick went in the other person? Did we flip a coin? Was it going to hurt?

"What's that?"

Oh, fuck.

My gaze landed on a pair of scuffed Adidas trainers, and I grimaced, forcing myself to look up. Yep, it was as I'd thought. Leo was staring at my phone screen with wide eyes. The phone screen which currently had a close-up of a guy with his fingers buried in another guy's ass.

I glanced around, and thankfully, we were alone for the moment. I had no idea where Connor and Niall were, but the important thing was that they weren't here.

What the fuck was I supposed to say to him without making it seem like I was expecting something to happen?

"It's just research."

"Research," he repeated slowly. When he lowered himself down next to me and tugged my phone from my unresisting grip, I fell back, throwing my hand over my face.

"You weren't supposed to see it."

The blanket moved beneath me, and warm breath skated over my ear. "Why?"

"Because I didn't want you to think that I was expecting we'd do...that."

He nudged at me with his head like some kind of overgrown cat until I moved my arm away from my face, and then he curled into me, pressing his nose into my neck as he liked to do.

"I've been doing some research, too," he confessed.

My heart beat faster. Curving my arm around him, I

stroked up the back of his neck and into his soft hair. "Yeah? The same kind of research?"

"Yeah," he mouthed against my skin.

Okay. We were on the same page, and most importantly, I hadn't scared him away.

"Did you come to any conclusions?"

He burrowed into me even further, pressing his face into the side of my throat. Stroking through his hair to soothe him, I waited until he'd relaxed before I tried again.

"Baby. Tell me."

His words were a soft whisper. "I think...I think I might want to try it with you."

My dick reacted *instantly*. Like he had a direct line to it. Reaching down to adjust it so it wasn't so obvious in my shorts, I groaned, unable to help my reaction.

"Fuck, me too."

"Okay. We, um, we should do that," he mumbled.

How could I feel so turned on and want to cuddle him at the same time? So sweet and so hot at the same time.

"Okay, I'm gonna pretend I didn't see Finn's boner. Niall?"

"See what? I didn't see anything. Nope. Not a thing."

Leo squeaked, scrambling away from me. I groaned, throwing my arm over my face and drawing up my legs, although there was no point in my doing so since apparently Connor and Niall had already seen it all.

"Where did you two go?" I asked, playing it cool despite my heated face and rapidly deflating cock.

When I lowered my arm, Connor jerked his head to the right. "We were interviewing the people with the campervan down the bottom of the field. Didn't Leo say?"

"I think they were a bit too busy for talking." Niall smirked, eyeing Leo, who was now sitting up with his legs pulled up to his chest and his arms wrapped around his knees. Leo glared up at him, but he was clearly biting back a smile. It helped me to relax a little. Maybe we were finally getting used to the teasing.

Still, I continued the discussion along project work-related lines. "Any new ideas for anything you want to add to your project?"

"Yeah." Connor flopped down onto the blanket in front of us and pulled out his phone. "I made some notes. First of all, we're gonna need to add options for electric and non-electric pitches..."

"Finn."

"Yeah?" I turned my head, my lips brushing over Leo's hair.

We'd arranged the tent so our camping mats were next to each other, and we'd unzipped the sleeping bags to use one as extra padding beneath us and the other spread out to cover us both. We'd topped it with an additional blanket in case it got cold during the night.

Although it was dark outside, thanks to the clear night and the brightness of the moon, I could just about make out the outline of his face as he continued. "You know the research we were talking about?"

"Yeah." I shifted closer, running my hand down his back. His bare back. The night was warm, and we were under two layers as it was, so we'd ended up in just our underwear.

"I really want to try it."

"Fuck." I let my hand slip lower onto his ass, and his breath stuttered over my skin. He rolled his hips forwards, dragging his hardening cock along my thigh, and as he slotted his leg between mine, I pulled him on top of me to get some friction on my own rapidly hardening erection. "I wish we could do it now, but I didn't bring any lube, and I don't think our first time should be in a tent. I want you to be comfortable."

He hummed against my throat. "Mmm. And you." Lifting his head, he kissed across my jaw, then the corner of my mouth, and finally, our lips met.

He pulled away, panting. Palming his ass as he rolled his hips down, I mouthed at the side of his throat. "Tell me what you'd do. If we could. I dare you."

"Finn. Oh, fuck." His soft little whimper made my dick throb. "More."

"You want more, baby? Tell me what you'd do." I eased down his boxer briefs as I continued kissing and licking over his skin. The way he was wriggling on top of me as he struggled to get mine off at the same time made my eyes roll back, my dick leaking precum. When Leo moved to straddle my thighs properly, letting them take his weight, I finally managed to get a hand wrapped around both of us. I'd seen someone do this in a video, and it had stuck in my mind, and I just hoped I could work out what I was doing so it was good for Leo.

"*Oh,*" he breathed. Shifting forwards, he brought his hand up. I couldn't exactly tell what he was doing in the dark, but I heard...was he spitting into his hand?

My question was answered a second later when his hand joined mine, sliding down our cocks, and it was wet.

I groaned. Why was that so fucking hot?

"I-I saw someone do that, when I was, um, researching," he whispered.

Words failed me. Thankfully, he didn't seem to expect a

reply, his hand joining mine in stroking our dicks together as he *carried on speaking.*

"If—if we could do it now...I'd want to be underneath you so I could feel you covering me. I'd feel safe."

"Oh, baby..." I stroked my free hand over his thigh.

"I don't know which way around we'd do it, but I'd want to make sure we spent enough time preparing. Before that, I think I'd like to kiss you. And...and for you to kiss me, and touch me, and—"

"Fuck," I gasped, my body seizing up as I came, hard, coating our hands in my release. Leo groaned, his cum-soaked hand moving faster on his own erection, and then he was coming, too, curling over me.

"More mess." His soft, breathless whisper was resigned, but I could hear the humour in his tone, and it made me smile. That, and the fact that we always seemed to end up with a mess to clear up.

This time, though, I was prepared. I manoeuvred him onto the camping mat next to me, missing the feel of his body against mine straight away.

"I brought wipes."

The noise that fell from his mouth could have been a question or agreement or something else...I didn't know. Concentrating on my goal, I dug out the pack of wipes and cleaned us up as best I could in the dark. When I'd done everything I could, the used wipes were safely stowed away, and we were back under the sleeping bag in our underwear, I pulled Leo into me, wrapping my arms around him.

"Are you okay?"

He nodded against me. "Yeah."

"Leo. I—"

The noise from outside had us both freezing up. I

couldn't describe it...something like the way I imagined a tent might sound if it was collapsing...

"Is that—" Leo began, but he cut himself off at the string of mumbled swear words in a familiar voice, followed by a sentence that I could make out clearly.

"We don't have a fucking tent, Con."

"Yeah, but—"

"Connor. Our tent collapsed."

"Yeah, and that's your fucking fault for not—"

"I've never been camping before! I've told you this a hundred times!"

"Okay! Fuck! We're gonna wake up the whole campsite if we don't shut the fuck up."

Their voices lowered, and I crawled to the front of the tent, unzipping the door flap. A rush of cool air entered the tent, and I shivered, although I did my best to ignore the sudden chill. What we'd done in this tent...let's just say it needed some fresh air to get rid of the evidence. It wasn't cold, anyway, just quite a bit cooler than the enclosed space where I'd been all wrapped up in my best friend.

"What's happening?" I hissed, and the two crouching figures in front of me startled.

"Someone didn't peg the ropes down," Connor ground out, and Niall huffed loudly.

"I told you, I didn't know."

"Yeah, and our tent collapsed." Connor paused for a moment. "Fucking hell," he wheezed, struggling against his laughter as it all sank in.

"Our tent collapsed," Niall screeched, and they both doubled over, falling onto the grass. I was so glad that we'd pitched our tents away from the other campers, although I was well aware that sound travelled at night.

"Hey! There are other people here," I reminded them,

and eventually, they got their laughter under control. I glanced towards where their tent had once been, the moonlight illuminating a sagging mass of canvas. Okay. It was clear they couldn't go back there.

"You'll have to sleep in our tent," I said eventually. It was the only option. The car was back in the tiny car park next to the farmhouse that belonged to the campsite owners, and there was no point in making them trek all the way there to have to sleep on uncomfortable car seats when I was sharing a four-person tent with Leo. Or at least, it had been advertised as a four-person tent when my parents had bought it. It was going to be a snug fit, but we'd make it work.

Connor pulled himself upright. "Your tent? Sleeping with you and your boyfriend?"

I sighed. "We're best friends."

"Best friends. Uh-huh." Niall clambered to his feet and then patted my shoulder. "Looks like we're all gonna become a lot more friendly in a few minutes." Without waiting for a response, he ducked into Leo's and my tent.

"Come on," I told Connor. "None of your shit is going anywhere. Your tent's a lost cause, but it's not windy or anything, so it'll all be there tomorrow."

"It better be," he muttered, but after grabbing his and Niall's sleeping bags and pillows, he followed me into my tent, where the four of us arranged ourselves as best we could. "Four person" was a definite lie. This tent had not been designed with four grown men in mind.

A bright light lit up the inside of the tent when we'd just settled down, with Leo curled into my right side and Connor to my left. I shouted, scrubbing at my eyes, Leo burying his face in my chest and Connor swearing loudly next to me.

"What the fuck, Niall?"

"Sorry, sorry. I had to get a picture of this for my girlfriend. She's not gonna believe it happened otherwise."

"Fuck's sake." Climbing over me and Leo, Connor swatted at him, and they tussled for a minute before collapsing into laughter again. Eventually, though, they quietened down, moving back to their original places. My body relaxed, and I absentmindedly stroked through Leo's hair while I closed my eyes, hoping sleep would come.

Words echoed in my mind.

Your tent? Sleeping with you and your boyfriend?

We were best friends. Not boyfriends.

Weren't we?

I fell asleep to the sound of Niall muttering that he hated camping, with the question still playing on my mind.

TWENTY-THREE

LEO

The email I'd received had taken me aback, and I wasn't sure exactly what had happened. I knew *someone* would have the answers, though, and so I pushed open the doors to the dance studio with more force than necessary, making both JJ and Alyssa flinch at the loud sound.

"Sorry," I said immediately because I hadn't meant to be aggressive. I just...needed answers.

Alyssa came up to me straight away, placing her hand on my arm. "Hey, Leo. Are you okay?" Her eyes were full of concern, and the guilt overtook me immediately. She wasn't involved in any of this, and the last thing I wanted was for her to be worried about me.

"Yeah, I'm okay. I just wanted to talk to JJ."

Her concerned gaze darted between me and JJ, but eventually, she nodded. "Coffee break, JJ? Let's all meet back here in fifteen minutes to rehearse."

I shot her a grateful smile as she ducked out of the studio, leaving me alone with my friend. Now we were alone, I found my nerves returning, but I pushed through.

"JJ?"

"Yeah?"

"Did you say anything to Dr.—Killian about my presentation?"

His mouth twisted. "Fuck, babe, I'm sorry. I know I shouldn't have said anything, but after what you told me, I needed to know if there was anything that could be done. Any provisions that could be put in place to make things easier for you."

I thought back to the conversation I'd had with him at our first dance rehearsal after the camping weekend. I'd been on a high with everything we'd achieved over the weekend, all the things we'd added that would make our project stand out. At the same time, I'd been filled with dread at the thought of the presentation. JJ had caught me at a weak moment, and the whole story had poured out of me. I didn't mind him knowing because he was my friend and already aware of my struggles.

Then, my lecturer had emailed me this morning, mentioning Dr. Wilder had some concerns about me doing the presentation...

Why can't I be normal? I asked myself for the thousandth time. It was fucking horrible feeling this way. On the one hand, I was grateful to my friend for caring enough to try and make my life easier—and for Dr. Wilder himself to do something—but on the other hand, angry with myself for yet again making my friends worry about me enough to go out of their way to try and make me more comfortable.

The result of JJ talking to his boyfriend-slash-scariest lecturer in LSU was that I'd discovered that the university had a policy in place for students who found it difficult to do presentations or speak up in front of people for whatever reason. I had no idea that was a thing until now. No one had ever told me, not that I'd ever communicated how difficult I found it to my lecturers. It was hard to explain if you didn't suffer from social anxiety, but suffice to say, I felt like I was a burden, and I couldn't even imagine feeling comfortable enough to speak to one of my lecturers about my issues.

"Leo. I was only trying to help, I promise. I'm sorry."

Shaking my head, I met JJ's gaze. "It's okay. I'm not angry, unless you count me being angry at myself."

JJ pulled me into a hug. "None of that. You know we love you, and we want to help you."

I sighed. "I know. I have to keep telling my brain that, but it doesn't always work."

He pressed a kiss to the side of my head before releasing me. "I know. Want to take your mind off it? I was inspired the other night at work, and I came up with some new choreo. I was discussing it with Alyssa before you came in, and we thought it might be good to try something a bit different."

"But you do sexy dancing at work."

"Exactly." He smirked at me. "Killian appreciated my moves—"

"No. I don't want to hear it."

"Babe, I'm just teasing you. It'll be sexy but classy, and I guarantee it'll push you out of your comfort zone. We don't need to perform it in front of anyone. Just for us. An added bonus for the significant others in our lives." The smirk was back, and I knew what he was referring to without him having to spell it out for me. Why did everyone think Finn and I were boyfriends? Okay, I knew why, but they were just seeing what they wanted to see. Finn and I knew the truth.

"Fine," I said eventually. "Let's do it." The part of me that was well aware of the effect my best friend had on me and vice versa was undeniably excited at the thought of performing it for him someday.

Wait a minute. I was looking forward to performing a routine in front of someone?

Whoa.

That was...unexpected.

Spinning to meet my own gaze in the mirrored wall, I squared my shoulders, holding my head high. "I'm going to do my presentation the same way as everyone else," I burst out, filled with a sudden rush of uncharacteristic confidence. I was certain I'd regret saying it later, but right now, I felt as if I could actually do it.

"Yeah, you are," JJ agreed, squeezing my arm. Behind us, the door opened a crack, Alyssa poking her head around the edge, and he beckoned her into the studio. "Who's ready to learn the hottest choreography LSU has ever seen?"

"This is ridiculous. I can't believe you're making me do this."

Finn gave me a crooked smile, and did he even know I'd do anything if he smiled at me that way, despite my own anxieties?

"I'm not making you. I'm daring you."

"Same thing."

He stared at me expectantly until I gave in. Glaring at him, I spun on my heel and stalked up to the bar, heading straight for the empty space right in front of the bartender. If only Charlie had been working today...but then, Finn would never have dared me to do this if Charlie had been the one at the bar. "Two shots of sambuca, please."

The bartender poured the shots quickly, and I focused on the flow of the liquid into the tiny glasses rather than my surroundings. Despite the fact I was here with Finn, my palms were clammy, and my heart rate was faster than usual. What had happened last time I was here at the student union...

"Here ya go." The bartender slid the glasses across the bar, and I tapped my card to the reader to pay. I even managed to give the guy a brief smile.

When I returned to Finn, I handed him his glass, and he knocked it against mine. "Ready to complete your dare?"

In reply, I tipped the shot to my lips and downed it.

"Oh, fuck!" I spluttered, wiping at my mouth frantically, tears coming to my eyes as I coughed. "I didn't know it tasted of aniseed!"

Finn was laughing so hard he had tears in his eyes. I elbowed him, and he stopped laughing, taking both our empty glasses and placing them on an overflowing table to our left. "Sorry. Your face!"

"You know I don't like aniseed."

He couldn't stop grinning, and I really didn't know why I liked him. "I thought it was like the time you said you didn't like Camembert, but then you tried it when my parents were having it, and you loved it."

Folding my arms across my chest, I stared him down. "I'd never tried Camembert before, though, so it was a guess. I *know* I hate aniseed."

"Aww, little lion." He slid around to my back, dipping his head to my ear. Curling his arm around my waist, he tugged me back against his body. "I'm sorry. I promise to never dare you to have anything aniseed-flavoured ever again."

I shivered as his lips skimmed my ear. "You'd better keep that promise. I can still taste it in my mouth."

He hummed against my skin. "How can I make it up to you? Want to dare me to do something?"

"You can get me a different drink to get rid of the taste." Sliding my hand down his arm that was wrapped around me, I threaded my fingers through his. He kissed the spot just below my ear and then brought his free hand up to cup my jaw, turning my head towards his.

"Hi," I said against his mouth.

"Hi."

Our lips met, so fucking softly, and my stomach filled with butterflies. Twisting around in his grip to give me a better angle to kiss him properly, I wrapped my arms around his shoulders, pressing another kiss to his lips. I took him by surprise because he staggered backwards, laughing breathlessly against my mouth as he let me press him up against the wall in our dark little corner of the bar. Drawing me closer, he coaxed my mouth open with more soft kisses, and when our tongues finally met, I didn't even mind the lingering taste of aniseed. I was so lost in Finn, and I never wanted to stop kissing him.

When we drew apart, he stared at me, his eyes huge and his pupils blown. "Fucking hell," he muttered, and I had to kiss him again. It was a compulsion. I could feel the growing bulge in his jeans, and I was in a similar state—which was still mind-blowing because I'd never really had to worry about anything like this before Finn had started having this effect on my body.

"Okay. We need—"

"To stop doing that before my situation becomes even

more obvious?" Finn grimaced, discreetly adjusting himself, and I cleared my throat.

"In case you didn't notice, you're not the only one."

He placed his mouth to my ear again. "I noticed. Don't worry, I'll do something about that later."

"*Finn*. Stop teasing me."

"Says the person kissing me and getting me into this state."

My brows rose. "It's my fault, is it?"

"Yeah." He threaded his fingers through mine. "C'mon. Enough distractions in a public place. We're here for your exposure therapy. I know we can't get rid of the bad memories from last time, but I'm gonna make sure you leave here tonight with a smile on your face."

"And no tears."

His lips curved upwards. "Unless you cry with joy over my insane kissing skills."

I punched him in the bicep, and he laughed, tugging me through the crowd in the direction of the room with the DJ. This was already so different from last time. I wasn't alone and scared, for a start.

Finn led me right into the centre of the dance floor, and I had a sudden flashback to that night. Standing there, alone and on the verge of tears, watching Finn so at ease and happy with his friends, talking to that girl...

"What's wrong?"

I blinked, realising I'd stopped dead, and Finn was eyeing me with concern.

"Nothing."

He shook his head, pulling me closer so he didn't have to speak so loudly over the music. "No, what is it?"

I knew he wouldn't drop it. Thankful that the darkness camouflaged the heat in my face, I leaned into him. "It's nothing, really. I was just remembering last time. I was standing at the side of the room watching you, and you looked really happy. You were talking to a girl—"

Finn's head shot up, his brows pulling together. His expression cleared after a few seconds, and he moved around me, wrapping his arms around my waist from behind, lazily moving us both to the music. I went with it, because, like pretty much everything else we did, it felt natural and effortless. Like it was a completely normal thing we did. Like there was no reason not to dance with him, right here, right now.

I felt his lips against my ear. "You know what I was talking to that girl about?"

"No."

"You," he breathed, punctuating the word with a soft kiss.

My body froze in place. "What?"

His thumbs caressed my hips before tapping lightly, and I took the hint, rolling my hips back in the lazy grind we'd fallen into.

"Yeah. I guess you didn't see, but I was talking to Charlie before that, and he mentioned that dance I did at Sanctuary, and, yeah...I got talked into doing a demonstration. Asha asked where I got my moves, and I told her all about how you taught me the dance and how you were an amazing teacher if you could make someone like me look good. Then, I told her how talented you were and how you could do anything you put your mind to." He huffed out a laugh against my skin. "Honestly, I think she got the impression I was obsessed with you. Although I guess I am your biggest fanboy, huh?"

I was warm all over, overflowing with it, happiness spilling out of me. This man. What was I supposed to say in response to that, other than I was so fucking grateful to have a friend like Finn?

It wasn't an exaggeration to say he was one in a million.

I loved him.

Whoa. Wait a minute.

I loved him.

TWENTY-FOUR

LEO

"It wasn't as bad as I thought it was going to be."

I stopped in my pacing to see Sam Payne, one of my classmates, leaning back against the computer lab's door frame with a relieved grin stretching across his face. Sam was one of the few guys I interacted with in my computing classes, and— Oh, fuck. He was kind of a friend, wasn't he? Why was I so bad at recognising the signs? Why did I always think the worst of myself?

"Your group presentation?"

He nodded. "Yeah. I couldn't sleep last night, worrying about it, but it went well, I think."

"*You* couldn't sleep?"

There must've been something in my voice because his brows rose. "Yeah, isn't that a normal thing when you're stressed about something?"

Maybe it was. "Uh...me too. I couldn't sleep, I mean."

"You'll be fine. It's honestly not as bad as you think." He pushed off the desk. "Good luck. You've got this."

I hoped with everything in me that he was right.

Connor and Niall entered the computer lab, closely followed by—

"Finn?"

He came straight up to me, pulling me into a hug. "Don't sound so surprised to see me. I wouldn't miss this."

"But—"

"But nothing. I'm here to support my best friend."

I love you.

I didn't say it aloud, but I wanted to, so badly.

"Thanks for being here," I said instead, burying my face in the crook of his neck and breathing in his spiced apple scent. My heart rate slowed straight away, his calming presence surrounding me. Last night, I'd decided to spend it apart from him, instead choosing to stay up late with Connor and Niall, going through every aspect of our project, the three of us quizzing one another until we knew the material inside out. Finn had texted me in the morning to wish me luck, but I knew he was supposed to be in a lecture right now. It hadn't occurred to me he'd come here instead.

But it should have, because of course he would. Because he was Finn Carsley.

Drawing back from me, he lifted the flap of the bag that was slung across his body. "Courtesy of my parents. Snacks for you all."

Connor and Niall crowded around him as he began handing out energy drinks and protein bars while I watched, unable to stop the huge smile that was overtaking my face. Finn caught my eye and gave me a soft, private smile, and I had to bite the inside of my mouth to stop blurting out the words I could never take back. Maybe I'd tell him someday, but today was not that day.

Somehow, the three of them managed to successfully distract me from worrying about the presentation, and in between Connor and Niall throwing sample questions at me and Finn constantly at my side, giving me small reassuring touches, the time passed quickly.

A beeping sound came from Connor's phone, interrupting his explanation of the additional options function, and we exchanged glances. It was time.

"Fuck," I whispered, squeezing my hands together in an effort to stop the tremors.

"Leo. Come here." Seated on the edge of one of the desks, Finn held out his hand to me. As I stepped up to him, he tugged me between his legs, his hands going to my shoulders and then rubbing up and down my arms. "It's gonna be okay, baby. I promise."

Leaning into him, I exhaled shakily, mumbling an apology against his shoulder. He sighed, wrapping his arms around me and pressing a kiss to the side of my head.

"There's nothing to be sorry for. This is why I'm here, and I'm not going anywhere."

Lifting my head, I met his gaze. "Thank you for being here."

"Always, baby."

Behind me, there was a loud sigh. "I feel so fucking single when I'm around you two."

I twisted in Finn's arms to see Connor pulling a sad face. Niall laughed, and Connor shot him a glare.

"Same when I'm forced to see you and your girlfriend, for that matter. Can all you couples fuck off?" His sad face disappeared. "Just kidding. You know I'm happy for you."

Another series of beeps came from his phone before any of us could reply, and I didn't know what I would have said.

Yes, I'm single...I think, but I don't know for sure. By the way, I think I might be in love with my best friend, and does that mean we're still friends, or are we boyfriends? How do I know? Help!

"Let's do this." Connor opened the door. "Good luck, guys."

"Good luck," I echoed, meaning it, and after Niall and Finn had returned the sentiments, we exited the lab. Swallowing hard, I stepped up to the lecture theatre door.

Finn stopped me with a hand on my arm. "You can do this. Remember, you're a Viking. My little lion." He leaned forwards, brushing a soft kiss across my lips. "I'll be right outside waiting for you."

I nodded, my nerves returning in full force, making my breath catch in my throat, but I held his words in my mind, letting them give me the courage to enter the lecture theatre. I could do this. I was Leo. *Lion.*

It was time I lived up to my name.

All the preparation we'd done had paid off, and when it came to my turn to present alone, my brain worked on autopilot as I went through the material and explained the reasoning behind my decisions, exactly as we'd practised.

Somehow, I made it through the entire thing without any major issues, despite my sweating palms and elevated heart rate. My hands shook, and I stumbled over my words several times, but I reminded myself to take deep breaths, telling myself that I could do this. Knowing that Finn was waiting right outside for me helped me to make it through.

The one thing my nerves hadn't let me do was to look at the people responsible for my grade. I knew it was probably better to make eye contact, but instead, I'd fixed my gaze on an empty row a little farther back in the lecture theatre. It might cost me percentage points when it came to marking my performance, but it was the only way I was able to make it through my presentation without falling apart.

When I finished, I dared to glance at my lecturer, and he gave me a tiny nod, which I hoped meant I'd done okay. The man next to him spoke my name, and I forced myself to meet his eyes, willing my impending panic away. This was the man who had introduced himself at the beginning as Dave Benson from Dataccelerate Consulting. He was the database expert and, therefore, was the person I needed to impress the most.

"Impressive work," he began, and my mouth fell open. I clamped it shut almost straight away, but the damage had already been done. The corner of his mouth turned up as I sucked in a shuddering breath. "I'd like to begin by asking how many rows are in your database and whether you envision any limiting issues in a live environment?"

My brain went offline. Completely and utterly blank. Fuck. Panicking, my gaze shot to Connor and Niall, seated at the side of the room. Connor subtly held up both hands, his fingers outstretched, and it all came flooding back to me. This had been one of the questions we'd rehearsed. I cleared my throat.

"F-for the testing environment, we designed it with ten thousand rows. In the—the live environment, we would host it on a bigger platform. Uh, so there would be scope to increase the database potential to a hundred thousand, which we calculated would give the booking site a ten-year lifespan, taking into account the occupancy rate and the number of rows needed for each customer's information. Th-that's including the booking extras."

Dave Benson nodded. Was that a good nod or a bad nod? Not allowing myself to panic, I turned my attention to my lecturer, who was asking me a question about the booking extras, and from there, the rest of the questions flew by in a blur.

When the three of us had been dismissed and we'd exited the lecture theatre, I fell back against the wall, closing my eyes. We'd done it. *I'd done it.*

A wild rush of adrenaline crashed over me like a wave. I felt invincible in that moment, like I could take on the world.

My eyes flew open as I was yanked into a hard body, spinning me around.

"You did it!" Finn shouted, a huge grin on his face.

"I love you," I breathed.

The world came to a standstill, and I was dizzy from being spun, so it took me a second to catch up. Finn was staring at me with wide, shocked eyes, his mouth open, and...oh.

Oh.

I'd just said those words aloud. Before we'd even had a chance to discuss whether we were still friends or maybe something different.

Alarms started blaring in my brain, and so I acted on instinct. I panicked, tearing myself away from him and making a run for it.

I didn't get very far. Finn's hand wrapped around my wrist, stopping me in my tracks. The next thing I knew, I was being dragged inside an empty classroom, the door slamming firmly behind us, with Finn blocking the exit.

"Leo."

I shook my head violently, glaring down at the floor and wishing more than anything I had a previously undiscovered superpower for burning holes through surfaces that would manifest right about now. It wasn't only my face that was on fire, it was my entire fucking body, and there was a lump in my throat threatening to choke me.

"Leo," Finn said again, and this time, his voice was so soft. He gently tugged on my wrist. "Look at me, please."

Forget the presentation. Meeting Finn's eyes was the hardest thing I'd ever done.

"Leo," he repeated, and his gaze was so serious my body trembled. "I want to dare you to do something."

I stared at him. *What?*

"This is a dare you can turn down, and I promise it won't affect our friendship either way. You're my best friend, and that's not going to change."

"W-what's the dare?" I whispered, my voice cracking on the words.

Pulling me closer, he brought his free hand up to cup my nape, his fingers sliding into my overgrown hair.

"My lion. You're so fucking incredible, you know?" He swallowed hard and then continued. "I...I dare you to be my boyfriend."

"Your boyfriend?"

"Yeah." The corners of his lips curved upwards. "I think...I think we might already be boyfriends."

Was this what it felt like to be high? I was floating, the warmth I'd felt earlier magnified by a million, spilling out of me as I lunged for Finn, throwing my arms around him and kissing him with everything I had.

When we broke apart, he laughed breathlessly, his eyes shining. "Was that a yes?"

"Yes. Yes. I accept your dare. I'll be your boyfriend," I said as seriously as possible, but I was smiling too hard for it to have the effect I was aiming for. "I was thinking the same thing as you. Or wondering. Whether we were boyfriends or if you even wanted that, or if—"

"I fucking want it, baby." His mouth slanted across mine again. "By the way, I love you back."

"You *what*?" I squeaked and then cleared my throat, attempting to speak at my usual lower pitch. "You do?"

"Yeah, I do. Fucking hell, Leo, you're everything to me. I knew it already, but I dunno, it didn't really register that what I was feeling was me in love with you because everything's just been..."

"Like a natural evolution?" I tried.

"Yeah, that." He gave me a soft smile. "So much. We somehow went from talking online to this, and I never even questioned it because it felt so right and so normal. Like it was meant to be."

"It was," I confirmed, making his smile widen, and it gave me the courage to continue. "You know you're my favourite person in the world, right?"

"Yeah. You're mine, too. No one else even comes close."

That declaration led to another kiss that got hotter and hotter, until a loud rapping on the door had us springing apart.

"Leo! Finn! Save it for later! We need to celebrate," Connor called through the glass, and I guessed the fun was over for now. Threading my fingers through my boyfriend's —*my boyfriend's*—I led us back into the corridor, where Connor and Niall were waiting.

"Finn's my boyfriend," I blurted out, still on a high and clearly not thinking straight.

Connor's brows rose, and Niall just looked confused.

"Yeah...we know," Connor said eventually. "That's old news. Why are you bringing it up now?"

"Uh..."

"Never mind," Finn said quickly after shooting me a sideways glance. "How and where are we celebrating?"

Niall jerked his finger toward the exit. "The student union because it's closest and we deserve drinks. We're starting with flaming sambucas."

I groaned. "Please, no. Anything but sambuca."

TWENTY-FIVE

FINN

"Mum, Dad, Ed...I have something to tell you."

My palms were sweaty as fuck. Why did no one tell me how nerve-racking it was to come out to your family? Yet, here I was, about to do it. I still wasn't sure whether to even put a label on it—bisexual, probably—but either way, the fact was that I was in a relationship with a man for the first time in my life. A man who happened to be my best friend, who was already considered part of the family. So...it wasn't like I *should* be afraid because I knew my family loved Leo, and I was sure they'd accept me. It was just...nerve-racking. Yeah.

Okay. Fuck it, I was just going to say it. "Leo's my boyfriend, and I guess I'm bi or whatever. The point is, yeah, uh, we're together." I cleared my throat. "He's my boyfriend," I repeated, as if there was a chance they hadn't heard me the first time when I'd practically shouted it across the kitchen table.

"Oh, sorry. Is this meant to be a surprise?" my dad said after an agonising silence that had Leo's breaths turning short and panicky next to me. Beneath the table, my hand found his, and I squeezed it gently, letting him know we were in this together.

"Bro, this is old news. I literally walked in on you two kissing." Ed rolled his eyes, and my dad laughed. I didn't know what my face was doing, but it made him laugh harder. Have you ever given your own parent the middle finger? I did, right then.

"Sorry. Did you want us to act like we're surprised?" He turned to my mum, widening his eyes and giving a fake gasp. "Can you believe it? Finn and Leo are in a relationship. They were *so* subtle. I never had a clue."

"Very subtle." My mum smirked, but then she pushed her chair back, coming around the table to stand next to me, placing her hand on my shoulder and squeezing lightly. "You know we love and accept you, whatever your sexuality. And, Leo—" She turned to him. "—you're part of our family, and we love and accept you, too."

"Thanks," he whispered, his lips curving upwards in a shy smile, and how was it possible for me to be so fucking head over heels for this person? And how hadn't I realised sooner?

Later, when we'd escaped to Leo's flat, after way too many intrusive questions from my well-meaning family, we stretched out on his bed, finally able to relax in our own private space. Leo curled into me, holding his phone out so I could see the screen.

"I told my dad about us. I-I didn't say I was bi because I don't know what I am. You know, I've only been kind of attracted to one other person, and that was a long time ago. So I just told him about you."

"Baby, it doesn't matter what you want to call it. The

fact is you're mine, and I'm yours, and that's all anyone else needs to know. We've said this all along. We don't owe anyone any explanations about our relationship."

He shifted forwards, pressing a kiss to my cheek. "I know."

When he laid his head on my shoulder, pushing his phone towards my face, I scanned the text thread with his dad.

LEO:

> Hi Dad. I tried calling a few times. I'm not sure when you'll be free to phone me back so I thought I would text. I wanted to let you know I have a serious boyfriend now. His name is Finn and he's a student at my uni studying engineering

> I hope you can meet him soon. He's amazing. I think you'll like him

It fucking hurt to see that Leo had sent those messages yesterday, after our celebratory drinks with Connor, Niall, and Niall's girlfriend, and he hadn't received a reply until this afternoon, just a couple of minutes before we'd sat my parents and brother down in the kitchen.

DAD:

> Good for you! Hope the course is going well. Keep up the good work

He'd added a thumbs up emoji, and that was the extent of their interaction.

There and then, I promised myself I was never going to let Leo feel like he didn't matter, that he wasn't important enough to answer the phone to. Leo was everything to me, and I was pretty sure he was aware of it, but just in case he wasn't, I was going to make sure I made it very, very obvious.

"It's good that he doesn't have a problem with me being with you, isn't it?" Leo murmured.

It's not good that he didn't bother calling back his own fucking son.

"Leo, you deserve so much more." Stroking my hand through his hair and then lightly scraping my nails over his nape, I sighed. "I am glad that he doesn't seem to have any issues with you being with me. I just wish..."

"I know. But I have you, don't I. And your family." His words were firm, stated as fact rather than as a question, and some of the tightness in my chest eased.

"Yeah. You have us, and you have our friends— Fuck. Speaking of our friends, when are we gonna tell them? And do you think they'll be as unsurprised as everyone else seems to be?"

Leo's laugh was muffled against my throat, his breath tickling my skin, making me laugh too.

"They've made comments about us being boyfriends before, so I don't think they'll be surprised. When do you want to tell them?"

I thought about it for a minute. "We're not acting any differently around each other, are we? Maybe we don't need an official announcement. Maybe we should just carry on as we are. Or..." An idea came to me, and a slow smile spread across my face. "What if we post some photos together? See how long it takes for them to notice."

It was a great plan, in my eyes. Not only would we get to troll our friends a bit—and they deserved it after all the boyfriend comments before they were true—but I'd also get to fill my camera roll with photos of my favourite person. Win-win.

"Oh. Okay, yeah." He pushed himself upright, sliding off the end of the bed. Eyeing me from beneath his lashes, he tugged his lip between his teeth, shifting on his feet.

"What is it?" I couldn't help smiling. He was so fucking cute when he went all shy.

"I wanted a photo of us for my phone wallpaper before, but I didn't know if we could do that."

"Of course we can do that. We could've done that before, too." Rolling off the bed, I crossed the room to his gaming chair and took a seat. I patted my thighs. "Come here, boyfriend. Let's get a photo of us looking all cute with our gaming headsets."

When we'd arranged ourselves with Leo seated on my lap and both of us with our headsets on, I leaned into him, hooking my chin over his shoulder, both of us smiling at the selfie camera. I took a series of photos, turning my head to kiss Leo's cheek in one of them, and then he twisted around, grabbed my head, and kissed my lips...

After that, we forgot all about the photos.

By the time I remembered what we'd originally been doing, we were on the bed, naked and breathless, coming down from the high of our orgasms, and my jaw was aching from sucking Leo's dick. Totally worth it.

When I'd regained the use of my legs, I recovered my phone and returned to Leo. We cleaned up, and then I pulled the duvet over us and wrapped my arm around him, so he could curl into me as we went through the photos we'd taken. I stopped on an image showing the two of us leaning into each other, the sides of our headphones pressed together. We were both grinning at the camera, our faces a little blurry where Leo had knocked my hand with his as I was taking the photo. Despite the minor blur, we looked so fucking happy, it was almost radiating out of the screen.

"This is the one." Opening my social media, I uploaded the photo, adding the caption "Gaming day with my favourite person," followed by a heart emoji, and then I tagged Leo's account. He only had a couple of posts on his profile, but I had the feeling that was about to change now we were officially together.

I was right...yet completely taken aback by what he did. Because I was scrolling through my notifications, I wasn't really paying attention when he reached for his own phone, and I was totally unprepared for the notification that appeared on my screen.

"You tagged me in a photo as well?"

"Yeah." Leo turned to kiss my cheek. "Look at it."

"Fucking hell, baby." I stared at the image on my screen.

"Too obvious?"

"Maybe, but I don't care." I placed my phone down next to me and then gently tugged his phone from his unresisting grip, placing it next to mine. "Come here."

Leo shifted onto me, his legs tangling with mine as his body pressed me down into the mattress. "Hi," he said, brushing his lips over mine.

"Hi. I love you."

His cheeks flushed. Dipping his head, he smiled against my skin. "I love you."

"That picture isn't gonna leave anyone with any doubts." I stroked my hand down his back. "It makes it all seem even more real."

"It is real. That's why I wanted to post the photo."

"Yeah," I said softly. "It's real."

Next to us, our phones lit up with notifications from our friends. The picture Leo had posted showed us lying in bed, with me scrolling through my phone with a grin on my face.

Leo was curled into me, smiling up at the camera. Only the tops of our upper bodies were in shot, and we were covered by Leo's duvet anyway, but it clearly showed that our shoulders were bare, and we were cuddling in bed together.

Leo had added a simple one-word caption.

Happy.

TWENTY-SIX

FINN

JJ's brows rose higher and higher as he took in the series of images on my phone screen. "What's all this?"

"I think it's obvious. I owed you a pair of trainers, so I want you to pick a pair, and I'll get them for you. I know you told me not to worry about it when I offered to replace them the first time, but...yeah. I know none of these are the same as the ones I ruined, but they're all really fucking expensive, so..." I trailed off with a shrug.

"Finn. I didn't—I was only joking about you ruining my shoes. Mostly. Yeah, I was pissed off at the time, but I'd never expect you to buy me a replacement pair. I should've known better than to wear them to a house party of drunk students."

I rubbed my hand over my mouth, staring down at the floor. This was more awkward than I thought it would be.

"Okay, I also get the impression you don't really like me, and I'm guessing you're not happy about the idea of me and Leo being together. So part of the reason I'm doing this is to—"

"Bribe me?" JJ finished.

"No! Uh, maybe, a bit."

He shook his head. "Look, just... Wait here." Jogging over to the entrance of the small dance studio I'd cornered him in, he closed and locked the door. When he returned to me, he lowered himself to the floor, his back against the wall, and tapped his hand on the smooth wood next to him.

I sat down beside him, pulling my knees up and resting my arms on them, a contrast to JJ's casual sprawl, his legs stretched out in front of him.

"I want to start by saying that I don't dislike you. Not at all. We don't know each other very well, and before you started hanging out with Leo, I didn't really know anything about you other than you were one of Ander's teammates who ruined my irreplaceable trainers. Then you were suddenly in Leo's life, and he...he was so fucking happy. Happier than I'd ever known him to be. More confident, too. He's still shy, but it's like he has a quiet determination inside him now that I've never seen before."

"He is happy. But that's all him. It's nothing to do with me."

"It *is* him, but what I'm saying is that him having your support means he's more comfortable expressing himself. The only thing I can feel towards you is grateful for the part you've played in helping him feel that way."

I let JJ's words sink in, but I couldn't quite believe them.

"That night at your house..."

"I was looking out for him. I wanted to make sure you had his best interests in mind, and now, it's clear to me you do." He turned to meet my gaze. "I'm happy he's with you. I trust you, and I know you won't knowingly hurt him, and I also know he's not afraid to speak his mind with you, is he?"

I shook my head. "We've always tried to be honest with

each other and talk things through. I trust him to do that with me, and he knows I'll do the same."

"Good. I don't want to seem like I'm being overprotective of him or pushy about your relationship because it's not my place. All I want is for him to be happy, and I know he is with you. That's all that matters to me."

"I love him so much," I confessed quietly.

JJ stared at me for a second, the corners of his lips curving up, and then he held out his hand. "Friends? Let's start with a handshake. We can work our way up to hugs."

I clasped his hand in mine. "Friends, and if you wanted a hug from me, all you had to do was say so. No need to hint."

"Babe. With all due respect, fuck off." He blew me a kiss with his middle finger, and I grinned. Yeah, he'd definitely forgiven me. Now, all I needed to do was get him to accept the trainers.

"About the Nikes—"

"I'm not letting you buy me replacements. I can't. It's too much."

"Just do it."

"No."

"Take them."

"No."

A loud banging on the door interrupted us before I could protest again. JJ rose to his feet in a smooth, graceful movement and glided over to the door, unlocking it and flinging it open.

"Hey, babe." He kissed Alyssa's cheek as she entered, her hands full with a large bottle of water, a towel, and her dance bag. My heart rate kicked up as I spotted messy red hair behind her, and then my boyfriend came into view, his green eyes sparkling and his lips curved into a sweet smile.

JJ pulled him into a quick hug as I climbed to my feet, crossing the studio in quick strides.

"Hi." I was sure I had a ridiculously huge grin on my face, but I couldn't help it. That was what seeing Leo did to me. Wrapping my arms around him, I pressed a kiss to his hair. "Missed you."

"Hi. I missed you, too. Are you going to tell me now why you had to meet JJ here without me?"

"I just wanted to straighten things out between us. He's one of your best friends, so I wanted to make sure we were on the same page with everything."

"You're the best." His lips met mine. "Best boyfriend."

I did not deserve this man. "Love you," I told him, because I could, and I didn't think I'd ever get tired of saying it.

"Love you." He kissed me again before stepping back. Biting down on his lip, he gave me one of his shy looks from beneath his lashes. "Do you have to be anywhere now? If you're not busy, you could stay and watch our dance practice. If—if you want to."

"Baby." I tilted his chin back up, my thumb stroking over his smooth jaw. "Of course I want to. If you don't mind me watching you, I'm all yours. Where do you want me to sit?"

His hand covered mine, and he tugged me towards the side of the studio, where there were a couple of folding chairs. Dropping his duffel bag on one of the chairs, he released my hand.

"Here." He waited until I was seated before continuing. "This is a work in progress, so bear that in mind, but I think you'll like it."

With those words, my boyfriend went from sweetly shy to sultry as fuck, with the sexy, heavy-lidded look he gave me, and my dick was not prepared to handle him throwing that kind of look at me in public. I rummaged around in his duffel as he strutted off to join JJ and Alyssa, pulling out his hoodie and balling it up in my lap, just in case. It was either that or potentially broadcast a boner to yet more of his friends, and I was still traumatised from Connor and Niall getting an eyeful during our camping trip.

You know how I'd just mentioned how my dick wasn't prepared? The music started up, and I didn't stand a chance.

The way Leo was moving made my mouth go dry. Fucking hell, he was so hot that I wouldn't have even been surprised to see flames appearing in the studio. Alyssa and JJ were probably hot too, but honestly, I couldn't even say because the only thing I could focus on was my sexy-as-fuck boyfriend.

By the time the dance finished, my dick was rock hard, and I was so. Fucking. Turned on. I needed to get Leo alone ASAP.

He prowled over to me like a lion hunting its prey, a hungry look in his eyes, and he'd never lived up to his name more than he did in that moment. When he reached me, he swung himself onto my lap, and I groaned at the sudden pressure on my erection.

"Oh, you liked it," he murmured, and all I could do was stare at him wordlessly because where had this confidence come from? It was so fucking hot.

"I loved it," I rasped. "And I need to get you home right now so I can show you my appreciation."

His tongue swiped across his lips as he placed his hands on my shoulders, leaning into me. "Let's go back to my flat."

Yes. Best idea ever.

"Now. Go now."

He suddenly broke character, tipping forwards and burying his face in the crook of my neck with a huff of laughter. "Sorry. I don't know how to do this sexy thing. I'm trying, but—"

"Leo. You don't even have to try. You are so fucking sexy. The way you moved during that dance...you were killing me. If we'd been alone, I wouldn't have been able to keep my hands off you."

He lifted his head, his eyes darkening. "Yeah?"

"Yeah. Now, do you have to practise anymore, or can we go?"

"Get out of here. We'll practise again tomorrow."

Leo and I both jumped at the voice next to us.

"JJ!" Leo burrowed into me again.

"Sorry, babe. Didn't mean to make you jump."

I could hear the smirk in his voice, and so I lifted my hand to give him the finger.

A laugh burst from his throat. "Seriously. Go. I'll text you, Leo. You did good today. Finn, I'm sure I'll see you around soon."

When he'd retreated to the front of the studio where Alyssa was stretching, I ran my hands up Leo's thighs.

"Wanna get out of here?"

"Yeah."

TWENTY-SEVEN

LEO

Showered and dressed in comfortable joggers and T-shirts, we were ready, and I couldn't delay any longer. Directing Finn to sit in my gaming chair, I navigated to my phone's music app and selected a song. Gathering my courage, I reminded myself that I was doing this for my best friend, the person I loved, who'd never judge me or make fun of me.

Then, I began to dance.

"Fuck, Leo," Finn groaned, his gaze turning dark and hot as I rolled my hips, doing a hybrid of the dance moves I'd practised with JJ and Alyssa and my own version of the choreo I'd watched online in preparation for this. Straddling his thighs, I lifted my T-shirt, tugging it up and off my body, leaving my torso bared to him.

"Can I touch?" he rasped, white-knuckling the arms of my chair, and I nodded. He inhaled sharply and brought his hands up, flattening his palms against my chest. His hands shook slightly, and it helped to relax me a little, knowing this was just as big of a deal for him as it was for me.

We both knew where this was going to end up, and I

couldn't lie to myself and say I wasn't afraid. I *was* afraid. But I was also excited that I was going to be experiencing this with Finn. I hadn't even thought I'd ever get to the point of wanting this with another person, but with him, everything was different. I wanted it all. I was greedy for Finn, and I wanted to try everything with him, to give him all my firsts.

He thumbed over my nipples, and my breath hitched, but I kept moving, rolling my hips down, watching as Finn's pupils expanded so the black almost completely obscured the deep blue of his irises, his cock lengthening and tenting his joggers. A gaming chair wasn't an ideal location for a lap dance, but we were both determined to make it work.

"Take it off," I murmured, running my fingers along the hem of his T-shirt, and he wasted no time in yanking it off his body, leaving all his gorgeous, toned muscles on show for me. Leaning in, I kissed across his collarbone and then up his throat. He moaned, getting his hands in my hair and tugging my head up so he could kiss me. The lap dance was forgotten as we lost ourselves in each other, kissing and kissing like we'd never get enough.

Was it possible to ever get enough of Finn Carsley?

He broke away, panting. "I want you so fucking badly. Do you want to try? If not, we can do whatever, I just—fuck, baby. I just want you so much, however you'll have me."

"I want to try." Sliding off his lap, I stripped off my joggers and underwear, no longer shy under his gaze, and he moaned.

"So fucking hot, baby. Get on the bed."

I got onto the bed.

Lying there, I watched him as he came to stand next to the bed, close enough to touch. It soon became clear that he hadn't bothered with underwear, his hard cock springing free as he lowered his joggers and kicked them away.

"Finn," I breathed, and he sucked in a shaky breath.

"I never knew it was possible to want someone this much." He glanced towards the newly purchased bottle of lube I'd left out on my bedside table. "How do you want to do it?"

So far, all we'd done was get lube and get tested at the sexual health clinic on campus. Obviously, I'd never done anything with anyone, ever—not counting the things I'd done with Finn, but I'd read some weird stories online that had made me paranoid. I'd forced myself to make an appointment to get tested, just to ease my mind, and I'd sat through a lecture about PrEP and STDs and some other acronyms I couldn't remember. Then afterwards, as I was leaving, the nurse had tried to give me a supply of condoms. Blame my anxiety or blame me for never knowing how to react in new situations, but I'd run out of there with my face on fire, clutching a handful of extra-safe condoms and hoping with everything I had that I didn't run into anyone I knew. Or anyone at all.

Anyway, the result of our trip to the clinic was us receiving the news that we were good to go. There was nothing stopping us from trying penetrative sex, other than our own minds. My mind, mostly, and I was pretty sure that a lot of Finn's apprehension was because he was worried about me.

"I...I don't know. What do you want?"

He shrugged and then laughed. "Fucking hell. Why don't we flip a coin? Heads, you top, and I bottom, tails the other way around?"

"It works for me. I thought you might dare me to do it

one way or the other," I teased, but he immediately shook his head.

"I wouldn't make that into a dare, not until we work out our preferences and comfort levels and everything."

"I know." Climbing onto my knees, I wrapped my hand around the back of his neck and pulled him into a kiss. "I trust you with my life, Finn."

"Same." He pressed forwards, his hard cock rubbing up against mine, making me moan. "You feel so fucking good, baby."

"Coin," I said breathlessly. "Quick."

"Yeah, okay. Yeah." Breaking away from me, he rubbed his hand over his mouth. "Coin. Right. Fuck. My brain goes offline when you start kissing me like that, and I can feel your cock against mine, like I can tell you're just as turned on as I am. It's just—fuck. Okay. Coin."

He turned around, and I was treated to a view of him from behind, of his muscles flexing as he moved to his wallet, digging out a coin. When he returned to me, I pulled him into another kiss. It felt like we both needed it.

"Okay. Let's do this. Heads, you top, and I bottom, tails, we do it the other way around. Yeah? Unless you wanna pick?"

"No, let's use the coin. Come on." It was my turn to press forwards, sliding my palms down his back as I mouthed at his throat. "I want this. I want you."

"Yeah. Yeah, okay. Me too."

His clear nerves helped to settle my own nerves in a small way, and I smiled, pressing one last kiss to his warm skin before trailing my nose up the side of his throat to his jaw, feeling the light scratch of his barely-there stubble.

"Flip the coin. I dare you."

That made him chuckle. "I accept the dare." He threw

the coin into the air and then slapped it down. When he lifted his hand, we both sucked in a breath.

Heads.

I was going to put my dick inside Finn.

"Uh." I cleared my throat.

"Yeah."

We stared at one another, and then both burst out laughing at the same time.

"How am I still this hard?" Finn eyed his dick with suspicion. "With all the nerves and talk about flipping coins, and now thinking about having your dick in my ass for the first time ever, it's a miracle."

"Mine, too." Wrapping my fingers around my cock, I stroked up the length.

Finn's eyes darkened. "Okay, I know why I'm still hard. Because you are so fucking hot. Lie back. Let's get comfortable."

We spent some time with me lying on top of him and then him on top of me, kissing, slowly grinding together until both of us were panting, overheated, and messy with precum smearing between our bodies.

"Lube," Finn breathed against my skin. "I wanna know what it feels like to have you inside me."

He rolled onto his front, and I reached for the lube, reminding myself that I was here with the man who loved me unconditionally, and it didn't matter if I fucked it up or even if he did. We were in this together. With that in mind, I pumped a generous amount of lube onto my fingers, clearing my throat as an indicator that I was ready. Finn spread his legs, and I carefully touched my finger to his rim.

He flinched, and I jerked my hand away, my heart pounding.

"Sorry!"

"No, no, it's okay. Just cold," he mumbled into the pillow. Turning his head, he gave me a shaky smile over his shoulder. "Keep going."

"Okay." Swallowing hard, I repeated my previous movement and began carefully circling his rim before daring to press the tip of my finger inside his hole. He exhaled slowly and deliberately as I pushed farther in, trying to remember the tips we'd read together.

When my finger was as far as I could get it, I paused.

"I-is that okay? I'm not hurting you, am I?"

"Feels weird, but it's okay. It doesn't hurt."

Stroking my free hand over the back of his thigh, I continued my movements, glacially slow, until Finn told me to add another finger. By the time I added a third, my movements were more confident, but my erection had flagged. I'd been concentrating so hard on whether I was opening him up right and if I was hurting him, I hadn't been able to focus on anything else. I knew his prostate was somewhere in there, but I hadn't even been able to think about trying to find it. Next time, if there was a next time, I'd make sure it was better for him. No one could be an expert on their first try, after all, unless they were some kind of prodigy or something.

"I think I'm ready now." Finn lifted his hips a little, pushing back against my fingers, and oh...there was something hot about the action that had my dick perking up again. Carefully withdrawing my fingers, I pumped a generous amount of lube into my palm and coated my cock, stroking up and down and feeling it harden beneath my grip. Fuck, I was about to have anal sex with my boyfriend.

"How should we do it?"

He shifted on the bed so his ass was at a higher angle as

he buried his face in the pillow. Mmm. It was a very nice view.

"Like this to start with. We can change if we don't like it."

"Okay. I'll, um, just put it in then." I lined myself up, holding on to him with one hand and circling the base of my dick with the other. The head touched his skin, leaving a shiny smear of lube, and he stiffened.

"Go slow."

"I will. Remember to breathe," I said, as much to myself as to him. Holding myself as still as possible, I made sure I was in exactly the right place, and when he exhaled, I pushed in.

Everything was so hot and so tight and like nothing I'd ever experienced before. Nothing that was even comparable to the previous experimenting we'd done. I kept pushing in, so slowly, both of us trembling. When I was all the way inside of him, I stopped, just breathing, thankful that I had an average-sized dick. And that Finn did, too, when it came to my turn to be on the receiving end. I imagined it would have been an even more daunting mission if I'd been on the bigger side.

"You're inside me," he whispered shakily, his hands flexing on the sheets.

"I'm inside you." I could see it and feel it, but I had to repeat the words for them to sink in. "I'm inside you. Is it okay?"

"Yeah. Just let me get used to it for a minute."

I used my minute wisely, stroking over the backs of his thighs and his ass, feeling him relax beneath me in tiny increments, the vice grip around my dick easing to a tightness that felt good.

"Okay. Try moving. Slow."

"Okay." Easing myself back, I gradually withdrew from him, getting about halfway before I pushed back in. "How's that?"

"Yeah. You can keep doing that."

After a few minutes of the same careful, shallow movements, we seemed to find our rhythm, Finn moving in time with my slow thrusts.

"I'm gonna try and get a better angle," he panted, and I slid out of him, letting him get adjusted. When I pushed back in, there was an immediate difference.

He groaned, and it wasn't a groan of pain. It was pleasure, and it was so hot.

"Fuck, baby. I think that was my prostate."

A smile spread across my face. "It was? Um, hang on, I'll try and do the same thing again."

It wasn't as easy as it seemed, but after a bit more experimenting, I was hitting more than I was missing, and Finn was making more of those sexy noises that were getting me hotter and hotter. So hot, I knew I was close to coming, but I really wanted him to come first.

"Finn. Close," I panted between thrusts. "Want you to—"

"Come in me, baby. Don't hold back."

It was as if his words had some kind of magic power because one minute, I was thrusting, the next, I was spilling inside him, gasping as my body shuddered through a climax that stole the breath from my lungs.

"*Finn.* Shit. Sorry." I was aware that I'd stopped thrusting, and I needed him to feel as good as I did.

"S'okay, baby. Fuck, you're so hot," he practically slurred into the pillow. "I'll finish myself off."

No. I wouldn't allow that to happen. Pulling out, I tugged at his hip, getting him to roll onto his back. Positioning myself between his thighs, I took his hard, dripping cock into my mouth without hesitation. As I did so, I pressed my fingers back inside him, aiming for his prostate.

I found it. The moan he let out seemed to echo in my ears as I sucked him in time with stroking over his prostate until his body tensed, and he came down my throat with a hoarse cry.

I was proud of myself for swallowing every bit of his cum, and afterwards, with blurry vision from my tears, gasping in a much-needed lungful of air, I collapsed into his arms.

When we'd cleaned up as best we could, I lay next to him, our heads sharing the same pillow.

"You okay, baby?" Finn pressed a kiss to the side of my head as he pulled the duvet up to cover us.

"Mmm. Good. You?"

"Good. We did well for a first try, didn't we? It wasn't as scary as I thought it was gonna be."

I shifted closer to him. "Yeah. You'll probably find it easier the other way around because you've done that before."

"Baby, no. That was nothing like this, and I don't even wanna think about anything else other than you and me. I'm gonna make it as good as I can for you, but of the two of us, you're the one who has experience with sticking your dick in someone's ass. You'll have to give me tips."

"Sticking my dick in someone's ass." Smiling, I turned to kiss his cheek. "That's such a romantic way of putting it."

"Oh, sorry. How about...inserting your sword into its sheath?"

"No." There was only one way to stop him talking, and that was to kiss his grinning mouth, so I attempted that, except I ended up kissing his teeth, which was kind of weird. Either way, it worked to stop him talking, and then he kissed me properly, a slow, deep kiss that made my toes curl.

"I wanted you to come from the sex," I said a little while later, when we were lying in each other's arms, trading lazy kisses every now and then.

"The way it happened was perfect." He drew back to meet my eyes, his gaze serious. "I don't want you to get in your head and think about how things could have been different. There was nothing I would have changed, and I got the bonus of the world's hottest blow job."

"It was really okay?"

His hand cupped my cheek, his thumb brushing over my bottom lip. "No, it was fucking exceptional. You're the best boyfriend ever."

My lips curved upwards. "You are. I love you so much."

He returned my smile, his gaze going so soft it gave me butterflies. "There's that smile I love. Love you so much, too, Leo."

I swallowed around the lump in my throat. "I'm so glad you started gaming with me."

"Me, too. Team Hammerking forever."

"Best team ever."

I fell asleep with the smile still on my face.

TWENTY-EIGHT

LEO

The stands were busier than I'd ever seen them. This was my first time at a home match, although I'd been to plenty of Finn's practices and away games, and as Finn had explained, the team was getting close to the end of the season. The players in their final year of uni would be gone once the semester was over, and that meant that the chances of watching this particular lineup play together were getting smaller with every match played.

"Wow. This is bigger than I thought it would be." Ed stared around us, echoing my thoughts exactly.

"It's not always like this," I told him, explaining what Finn had told me about the end of the season and the players leaving. He shook his head as we took our seats, kicking his legs up to rest on the low barrier that separated the front row from the pitch.

"I used to watch Finn at school sometimes. He's four years older than me, but when I was in year seven and just starting at our senior school, he was in year eleven, and it was so cool having this older brother who was amazing at football and who everyone liked. I used to sneak into his matches and watch from a distance so he didn't have his annoying little brother distracting him."

I glanced over at Ed. "No, that's not true. He loves you being there for him."

"Maybe now. Not then."

I couldn't respond to that with any accuracy because I hadn't known either of them back then, but what I did know was that Finn loved his brother and parents, and they loved him in return. They had such a close bond, and I still couldn't get my head around the fact that they included me as part of their family. My relationship with my dad wasn't ever going to be like the one Finn had with his mum and dad, and I'd made my peace with that a long time ago. Yet, somehow, I'd ended up with another family of my own—not replacing what I had, but adding to it, giving me two extra parents who genuinely cared about me and a surrogate younger brother who seemed to be able to gauge my moods and knew when to tease and when to back off. It was so much more than I could have ever dreamed of. With Finn, I hadn't only gained a boyfriend. I'd gained a family.

"All kids are annoying in their own way," I told Ed, doing my best to reassure him. "Finn was excited that you were coming to watch him today."

Ed shot me a quick grin before returning his attention to the pitch, which was currently empty. "I hope so."

"It's true. He told me to watch out, though."

"For what?"

"You, flirting with girls."

Ed laughed. "Yeah, fair enough. If they're hot, though, I'm gonna try my luck."

"Um...okay."

"Leo!"

I turned just in time to see Niccolò launch himself at me, laughing into my ear as I caught him, spinning him around. We'd become close friends lately, which wasn't something I'd thought would happen in the past, with his loud, outgoing personality the antithesis of my shyness and anxiety around people. But somehow, it had, our friendship cemented after that night in the student union.

In fact, my friend group had widened to include not only Niccolò but also his boyfriend, Bennett, and several of Finn's teammates and their partners. Noah, especially. We'd originally bonded over *Mario Kart*, and I'd even played him one-on-one a few times when our boyfriends had been busy with football training.

Speaking of... "Hi." A grinning Noah lifted his hand in a wave as he slid into the seat next to Nic's, closely followed by Elliot.

"Where are the girls?" Ed pouted as I returned Noah's greeting.

Nic jabbed him in the bicep with a perfectly mani-cured, glittery blue fingernail. "Girls? Boys are better. All those lovely manly—"

"Debatable." Ed cut him off with a swift shake of his head before his attention was drawn to someone behind me. His eyes widened. "Now that's what I'm talking about. Leo, be my favourite big brother and get me an intro with her. Or one of her friends."

My brows rose. "Have you met me? I'm the least likely person to introduce myself to anyone new."

"I'll do it." Niccolò followed his gaze. "Ooh, pretty. You have good taste for a straight boy."

"Don't encourage him," I mumbled, but neither of them

was listening to me, whispering and giggling. I forced myself to turn around to see—

"Millie."

"Leo."

We both spoke at the same time, and Millie smiled widely while I gave a nervous laugh. Finn and I had played online with her and Daisy several times since the initial time we'd played a quad campaign, and although I still struggled to speak to either of them outside of the game environment, our shared love of *Lesath Legends* gave us enough conversation topics that I was able to get by.

"Ahem." Ed cleared his throat loudly, elbowing me in the side unsubtly.

I sighed, my gaze flicking to Millie's companions. "Ed, this is Millie, Daisy, and Sophie. Everyone, Ed is Finn's younger brother."

He grinned widely and then winked, which I honestly didn't think people did in real life. Maybe he had something in his eye. "Which of you beautiful ladies are single and want some quality one-on-one time with the hottest Carsley brother?"

I covered my mouth with my hand to hide my smile, and Nic leaned up to whisper in my ear. "Watch out for this one. He's as forward as I am."

"I can see that."

Millie was eyeing Ed with amusement. "How old are you?"

"Sixteen, seventeen in a few months. And alllll man where it counts."

"Please, make it stop," I whispered to the sky.

"Hmm." Millie tapped her lips. "How about this? If you're still single when you're eighteen and you decide to go to LSU, come and find me. I'll see about introducing you to my cousin. I think you'll like her."

"It's a deal. Take care, ladies. Have a great day." He blew the three of them kisses, and when he'd turned to face the pitch again, I stared at him.

"Who even are you?"

"I'd say I'll give you some tips, but my brother would kill me. Plus, I don't want you two to ever split up." His eyes widened. "Fuck! That never even occurred to me until now. Please, never split up. I'm begging you." He placed his palms together in a praying motion, sticking out his bottom lip. "I wanna be best man at your wedding. Can I be best man? Wait, how does it work with two men? Do you get a best man each? Can I be yours? Oh, but then Finn would be sad. Maybe I could be yours for half the wedding and Finn's for the other half?"

"Ed."

It was the only word I managed to say before Nic was barging in between us, grasping Ed's arm.

"We could theme the wedding," he gasped dramatically. "A gaming theme! But not tacky or anything."

"Please make it stop," I begged the sky again, my face heating, and it wasn't from the sun. Closing my eyes, I did my best to tune out what was now an animated discussion of my completely hypothetical gaming-themed wedding, pretending I was anywhere but here.

"Leo?"

My eyes flew open to see Finn standing on the other side of the low barrier, looking gorgeous in his football kit.

I blinked, hoping he wasn't a mirage I'd conjured up in my efforts to tune out the conversation that was still happening to my left.

"Leo? Baby, what's wrong? Come here."

I took the couple of steps forward that took me to the edge of the barrier, and he instantly wrapped his arms around my waist, pressing a soft kiss to the tip of my nose.

"Hi," I whispered. "Your brother and Niccolò are planning our wedding."

"They what?" he screeched, jumping back, his gaze flying to Ed and his co-conspirator.

"Yeah." I sighed. "According to them, it's going to be gaming themed, and Ed wants to be my best man half the time and yours the other half."

"Is that so?" His initial shock faded away, replaced by amusement. "Where did this all come from? Is Niccolò influencing my brother?"

"What's going on?" Bennett jogged over, coming to a stop next to Finn. "I heard my boyfriend's name mentioned."

"Apparently, he and my brother are planning our wedding." He shrugged, smirking at his teammate. "I dunno about you, but it sounds like your boyfriend has marriage on the brain."

"Don't start," Bennett warned him, his voice stern even though he was biting back a smile. "Do I need to remind you we're still students, and not only that, not all couples get married?"

"Even so, you're the one with the wedding-obsessed boyfriend."

"Fuck off."

They elbowed each other, grinning before a whistle sounded behind them.

"Gotta go. Wait for me afterwards, okay?" Finn kissed me softly. At his side, I was dimly aware of Bennett doing the same with Niccolò, but I only had eyes for one person.

"Good luck. Win the match." I pressed another kiss to his lips before he stepped back. He nodded, giving me a bright smile.

A throat cleared next to me. "Yeah, good luck. Kick their fucking asses!"

Finn turned to his brother. "Thanks. I'll try. Glad you're here."

Ed smiled, shooting him a thumbs up, which he returned before he gave me one final quick kiss, and then jogged away.

"Remember when you were pretending you two were just friends?" Noah teased me as Finn lined up with the rest of his teammates.

"OMG, bro, you should've seen Finn when he sat us down in the kitchen. All fucking dramatic, like he was gonna tell us something serious, and then he was all like, Leo's my boyfriend, as if we didn't know. I'm like, bro, I literally walked in on you dry humping, and I can never unsee that."

"You did not!" I placed my head in my hands. "I hate you all. I miss the days when I had no friends."

"Does my brother know he's dating a liar?" Ed wondered, and then he threw his arms around me before I had a chance to respond. "I'm just kidding. You love us really, don't you?"

"I guess so," I mumbled from behind my hands. "Please stop embarrassing me, though."

"Sorry," he said sincerely, and I lowered my hands.

"It's okay. I'm just...you know."

"You're Leo, and we love you, and we don't want you to change."

"That," Nic said, sliding his arm around my waist.

As the whistle sounded to begin the match, I smiled.

I'd come a long way from that shy, stuttering little boy who wanted nothing more than to hide away from the world. It didn't matter if I wasn't magically cured of my shyness. I had people around me who understood. People who were my friends.

I was a lucky, lucky man.

TWENTY-NINE

FINN

"I've been thinking about this all day." I ran my hands down Leo's back and onto his ass, earning me a shuddering breath exhaled against my throat, followed by the light scrape of teeth. Fucking hot. I had my boyfriend naked in my arms, and I was about to fuck him for the first time.

I'd bottomed for him a few more times since we'd first done it, but generally, we'd stuck to blow jobs or hand jobs or frotting against each other until we came. All of which were amazing, and even if we'd never done anything penetrative again after the first time, I would've been happy. I knew Leo had been apprehensive about bottoming, and I hadn't ever pushed it, but he'd been the one to bring it up early this morning, both of us caught in that state between dreaming and awake, when nothing seemed real. With his arms wrapped tightly around me, he'd told me in no uncertain terms that we'd made an agreement to try it each way, and it was happening—if I wanted it to happen.

Yeah, I wanted it to happen. I was really fucking nervous about messing it up, though. Now we'd done it a few times, I had more of an idea about how it might feel for him, but I wouldn't be able to tell for sure. I'd be relying on verbal and visual cues, and I just hoped I could read him well enough to know how to make it good for him.

"I've been thinking about it all day, too," Leo murmured, mouthing over my pulse point. "I want to know how it feels." He lifted his head, meeting my gaze. "I-I'm scared, but I'm excited. I trust you."

"I love you so fucking much." Palming his ass, I pulled him closer, our hard cocks brushing together as he pressed against me.

"I love you. I want you so much," he said so quietly, his cheeks flushing. I kissed each cheek, then his nose, and then his gorgeous lips. His mouth opened for me straight away, our tongues sliding together and then away, my teeth lightly scraping over his bottom lip as I fumbled for the lube one-handed and then pressed my slicked-up finger to his hole.

I kept kissing him as I eased my finger inside, and he kissed me back almost desperately, holding me so tightly as I pushed it in all the way, only breaking our kiss with a breathy "More."

Opening him up as slowly and carefully as I could while he moaned into my skin and rolled his hips down, his hands all over me as his lips connected with mine again and again, was the biggest torture I'd ever experienced. It was as if he knew exactly what to do to drive me wild, and by the time he was ready, my cock was dripping with precum, so hard and aching.

A memory flashed through my mind. Leo, back when we were camping.

If—if we could do it now...I'd want to be underneath you so I could feel you covering me. I'd feel safe.

"Baby." Fucking hell, my voice was so raspy. "Want to lie down?"

He blinked at me, all glassy eyes and blown pupils. "N-no. Yeah. I mean, I do, but not yet. I want to try...let's start off like this." Rising onto his knees, he positioned himself over my dick, and I wasted no time in lubing it up and holding it in place.

And then. Then, he was moving down, down, down, encompassing my erection with his hot body, his face screwed up in concentration as he lowered himself all the way.

"*Fuck,*" I gasped, a myriad of sensations overtaking me. So hot, tight, so fucking sweet, and when he rose again, riding my cock like a fucking pro despite it being his first time, I had to bite down on the inside of my mouth. The sting of pain kept me grounded, and as I snapped my hips up to meet his, I was glad for it because his breathy moan would've sent me over the edge otherwise. This was nothing like I'd imagined and way more than I could've ever imagined at the same time.

His hips came to a stuttering halt when I wrapped my hand around his cock.

"*Oh.* Fuck. Finn. Can we do it the other way now? Lying down?"

"Course we can."

When I withdrew from him, my dick throbbed, and I knew that if Leo's experience was anything like mine, he'd be feeling empty, craving to be filled again, and so I got us into position as quickly as I could. When Leo was beneath me, his hips angled upwards with a pillow propped underneath them, I pushed back inside, both of us groaning at the feeling as I re-entered him.

I covered his body with mine, relishing the feel of his warm skin, his shifting muscles, and his hard cock between us. Thrusting in and out of him, encouraged by his moans, I kissed him, messy and uncoordinated, as his hips rose to meet mine, and we panted into each other's mouths.

"Touch...touch yourself," I ground out between kisses, and he got his hand down between us, his fingers rubbing against my torso as he curled them around his cock. My hips snapped forwards, and he cried out, his hand working his length as it pulsed between us, his cum hitting my abs and smearing over our skin as we moved together. When he sucked in a shuddering breath, I pulled out, stroking my cock hard and fast as I took in his fucking sexy body covered in cum, and it felt like only seconds before my cock was jerking in my grip, my release joining his, painting his skin, marking him as mine.

Mine.

Leo was mine, and I was his. How had I managed to get so fucking lucky? To find someone that fit me so perfectly when I hadn't even been looking for them?

"Leo?"

"Mmm?" My sleepy boyfriend hummed against my chest, his body lax in my arms. It had been a long day and an even longer night, and after dragging ourselves through the routine of showering and getting ready for bed, we were ready to collapse. Both of us were on the verge of sleep, but I wanted to get the words out before we succumbed.

"Thank you."

"For what?" He shifted closer, his thumb stroking over my side.

"For being you. For trusting me with the important things. For being so easy to fall in love with."

"Finn. Baby," he whispered, and the fact that he never

called me by any nicknames made the moment all the more special. I swallowed around the lump in my throat as he continued, his words thick with sleep but so, so sincere. "Thank you for making my life so much better. Everything's better with you. I love you more than I could have ever imagined loving anyone."

I pulled him into me, as close as I could get him. "I feel the same."

"I forgot to say." Stifling a yawn, he stretched and then curled back into me. "I got the results back from my project presentation today. Seventy-eight percent."

"Baby, that's amazing." I was so happy for him. "I knew you could do it."

"You helped."

"No. Leo, that was all you. You impressed the panel, you put in the work...*you* did that."

"I did, didn't I?" Despite the obvious disbelief in his voice, there was a note of pride.

"You did. You're incredible. Whatever you put your mind to, you achieve."

"You make me sound like one of the *Lesath Legends* heroes," he said softly.

I shifted until I could meet his gaze.

"You *are* like one of those heroes. You're Leo Evans. My lion."

A slow smile spread across his face, even as his eyes filled with tears. He reached out, tracing a finger across my jaw. Cupping my cheek, he moved closer until our foreheads were touching, his warm breath skating across my skin.

"Your lion," he said.

LEO

EPILOGUE

FIVE YEARS LATER

"Surprise!"

Three voices shouted at the same time as Finn lifted his hands from my eyes. I blinked at the sudden rush of light in my vision, but it only took a few seconds for the world to come into focus. Finn's parents and Ed were standing in the kitchen behind the table, which was piled high with all my favourite foods, including several giant pizzas. A "congratulations" banner hung from the ceiling, and several helium-filled balloons were bobbing up and down, tethered to various surfaces with shiny ribbon.

"What? This is for me?"

Arms wrapped around my waist from behind, and a soft kiss was placed to the back of my neck before Finn hooked his chin over my shoulder.

"All for you. We wanted to celebrate your promotion."

"Database engineer at Lightdark Studios. That's the coolest job ever, especially for you since they produce your favourite game." Ed rounded the table to throw an arm around us both, squeezing my shoulder. His other hand was occupied with scooping up a huge slice of pizza, which he attempted to shovel into his mouth as he was hugging us. Finn pushed him away, muttering about chewing sounds, and they began bickering good-naturedly as I headed over to their parents.

"Congratulations." Finn's mum hugged me, followed by his dad. "We're so proud of you."

"Thank you." I smiled at the two people who had become my surrogate parents. My dad had his own life, and although we kept each other updated on the important things and met up when we could, I'd never have the close relationship I had with the Carsleys. "I can't believe I got the job. I thought someone with more experience would get it."

"Don't downplay your talent." Finn pressed up against me again, wrapping me up in his arms and surrounding me with his spiced apple scent. "You're amazing."

"You are, Mr. Biomedical Engineer. *That's* impressive."

"That's old news." He kissed the spot just below my ear. "I don't get to work on our favourite game every day, do I?"

"It's not as exciting as you make it sound," I said. It was true because my job wasn't the most glamorous, but it was an important part of the whole game creation process. I got to work in a relaxed environment where I helped to develop the game I loved without having too much human interaction. My social anxiety wasn't ever going to go away, but my bosses understood how I was, and most importantly, it didn't affect the work I did.

I got to do a job I loved, Finn got to do a job he loved, and we got to come home to each other every day.

It might not have seemed like an exciting life to some people, but to me, it was everything. We had a small flat in south-east London that we called our own and had decorated together, with the second bedroom converted into a gaming room, and we had the rings we'd chosen on our left hands as a symbol of our commitment to each other.

Yes, we were married. It would be our one-year wedding anniversary in two months.

No, we didn't have a gaming theme for our wedding.

Okay...that wasn't strictly true. We had a *Lesath Legends*-themed wedding cake. A nod to the way we'd met.

Want to know how I proposed to Finn?

It happened after a long night of gaming, with us curled up in our bed, having pushed aside his controller and my computer keyboard and mouse. We'd just successfully completed our final campaign, and we were both on a high. The curtains were open, the first rays of the morning sun struggling to pierce the clouds, dimly illuminating the street outside our window in a soft, hazy light.

I looked at Finn to find him already looking at me, his eyes shining, reflecting everything I felt for him right back at me, taking my breath away.

The words had just come out, completely unplanned, but so easily, just like everything else between us.

I dare you to marry me...

THE END

THANK YOU

Thank you so much for reading Finn and Leo's story! The final book in the series, Matched, is available for pre-order now at https://mybook.to/LSUmatched

Are you interested in reading more from some of the other characters in the series? Check out the following:
    Collided (Cole & Huxley) - prequel
    Blindsided (Liam & Noah)
    Sidelined (Ander & Elliot)
    Ignited (JJ & Killian)
    Tempted (Bennett & Niccolò) - novella

If you want to know what else is coming up, sign up to my newsletter for updates or come and find me on Facebook, Instagram, or Patreon. Check out all my links at https://linktr.ee/authorbeccasteele

Becca xoxo

ONE MORE THING...

Social anxiety can be a real struggle. Sometimes the support of family or friends can help, and there are lots of other resources out there such as therapy, helplines, online tools to learn coping techniques, forums where you can connect with other people going through the same issues, etc. I wanted to share a few of the tools I've found helpful and are easily accessible online, in case they're useful to anyone:

Finch—a free self-care app for Android and Apple
Headspace—a meditation app for Android and
Apple
Reddit:
r/Mindfulness
r/socialanxiety

If you can relate to Leo, just know that you're not alone. And if you can relate to Finn, the world needs more people like you.

ACKNOWLEDGMENTS

While I'd decided that Finn was going to get his main character moment as part of the LSU series, I hadn't originally planned on giving Leo a story. As I was writing Ignited and I started to get to know him as JJ's friend, I fell in love with him, and instantly knew he would have a connection with Finn. I couldn't wait to find out how it would all happen, and how two seemingly different people could form this amazing, unshakeable bond. I'm so happy that they got their story and well-deserved HEA, even if it took them a while to get there...and everyone else knew before they did...

Now, I need (and want!) to thank a few people who were instrumental in helping their story come to life. First of all, thank you to Claudia and Jodi, who let me share all of my random ideas and encouraged me when I was down, and are just the best cheerleaders. I love you! And of course, Jenny for being amazing as always, and Amy for all your support and insight. You guys are awesome and so appreciated!

To Ivy, Blake, and IA, thank you for our sprint sessions —this book wouldn't have been finished on time without our mornings battling monsters while trying to get as many words written as we could.

My amazing Patreon readers, my blogger and ARC teams, Jen, TAA & Wordsmith, and the book community—I love and appreciate all the support, reads, reviews, recommendations, promo, edits etc.

And of course, a huge thanks to Sandra and Rumi for helping me to get Dared into a publishable state! Sorry for my excessive use of em-dashes (but you know I will never, ever give them up).

Finally, thank you so much for taking the time to pick up this book and read Finn and Leo's story. It means a lot to me, and I hope they brought some happiness to your day.

Becca xoxo

The Bonds We Break

The Darkness In You

Alstone High Standalones

(new adult high school romance)

Trick Me Twice (M/F)

Cross the Line (M/M)

In a Week (M/F short story)*

Savage Rivals (M/M)

London Players Series

(M/F rugby romance)

The Offer

London Suits Series

(M/F office romance)

The Deal

The Truce

The Wish (festive short story)*

Other Standalones

Cirque des Masques (M/M dark circus romance)

Reckless (M/M soccer romance)

Mayhem (M/F Four series dark spinoff)*

Heatwave (M/F summer short story)*

After Dark (MMM Cirque des Masques short spinoff)*

Boneyard Kings Series (with C. Lymari)

(MFMM why-choose college suspense romance)

Merciless Kings

Vicious Queen

Ruthless Kingdom

Blackwell Lake Series (with C. Lymari)

(MMMF why-choose college suspense romance)

Beneath the Surface

Box Sets

Caiden & Winter trilogy (M/F)

(*The Four series books 1-3*)

*starred books (plus bonus scenes) are available as free downloads from https://authorbeccasteele.com

**Key: *M/F = Male/Female romance | M/M = Male/Male romance | why-choose = one woman & 3 men romance (also known as reverse harem)*

Within Becca's why-choose books, MFMM indicates that all men have a relationship with the woman, but do not interact with each other sexually or romantically. MMMF indicates that all parties interact sexually and romantically

ABOUT THE AUTHOR

Becca Steele is a USA Today and Wall Street Journal bestselling author of new adult romance from contemporary to dark. Her books have been translated into multiple languages.

Becca resides in the south of England with her family. When she's not writing, you can find her reading or gaming. Failing that, she'll be watching Netflix or curating yet another Spotify playlist.

Join Becca's Facebook reader group Becca's Book Bar, sign up to her mailing list, check out her Patreon, or find her via the following links:

facebook.com/authorbeccasteele

instagram.com/authorbeccasteele

bookbub.com/profile/becca-steele

goodreads.com/authorbeccasteele

patreon.com/authorbeccasteele

amazon.com/stores/Becca-Steele/author/B07WT6GWB2

Printed in Great Britain
by Amazon

58189864R00169